# HOLY LANDS

# HOLY LANDS

*A Novel*

**AMANDA STHERS**

BLOOMSBURY PUBLISHING
NEW YORK • LONDON • OXFORD • NEW DELHI • SYDNEY

(Translation of *Les Terres Saintes*)

BLOOMSBURY PUBLISHING
Bloomsbury Publishing Inc.
1385 Broadway, New York, NY 10018, USA

BLOOMSBURY, BLOOMSBURY PUBLISHING,
and the Diana logo are trademarks of
Bloomsbury Publishing Plc

First published in the United States 2019

*Les Terres Saintes* copyright © Amanda Sthers, 2010
Translation copyright © Amanda Sthers, 2019

ISBN: HB: 978-1-63557-283-4; eBook: 978-1-63557-281-0

Library of Congress Cataloging-in-Publication Data

Names: Sthers, Amanda, 1978– author, translator.
Title: Holy lands : a novel / Amanda Sthers.
Other titles: Terres saintes. English
Description: New York : Bloomsbury Publishing Inc., 2019.
Identifiers: LCCN 2018015184 | ISBN 9781635572834 (hardcover : alk. paper) |
ISBN 9781635572810 (ebook)
Classification: LCC PQ2719.T44 T4713 2019 | DDC 843/.92—dc23
LC record available at https://lccn.loc.gov/2018015184

2   4   6   8   10   9   7   5   3   1

Typeset by Westchester Publishing Services
Designed by Sara Stemen
Printed and bound in the U.S.A. by Berryville Graphics Inc., Berryville, Virginia

To find out more about our authors and books visit
www.bloomsbury.com and sign up for our newsletters.

Bloomsbury books may be purchased for business or promotional use.
For information on bulk purchases please contact Macmillan Corporate
and Premium Sales Department at specialmarkets@macmillan.com.

# HOLY LANDS

# From Harry Rosenmerck to Rabbi Moshe Cattan
Nazareth, April 1, 2009

Dear Rabbi Cattan,

I've followed all of your instructions ever since moving to Israel to breed pigs. I put them in a stilt pen over the sea just like the Hawaiians do. Not a single hoof will touch Holy Ground. Except, of course, if you agree that we should use them to hunt down terrorists. (Incidentally, I saw a photo in the *New York Times* last month of a soldier from the IDF with a pig on a leash and, frankly, I think it discredits our reputation for being hard-core!).

I have a deep respect for religion, even if I don't really practice it, and I never meant to upset you.

Also, I found your letter a little harsh, and calling me a "son of a bitch" won't change the fact that Israeli Jews can't seem to get enough of bacon or that I sell it to them in a restaurant in Tel Aviv, by the way.

Personally, I don't eat any since it's too high in fat for my already high cholesterol. I'm just trying to make a living. If I don't sell them pig, they'll just go and buy it from a goy. Eggs and bacon are on the menu and there's nothing you can do about it. They think it's elegant, like chicken potpie or frogs' legs.

What's the story with pig blood, Rabbi? You remember the brilliant idea to hang blood bags inside city buses so any terrorists who wanted to blow themselves up would be covered in it and made impure? So they wouldn't get into Paradise with the seventy-two virgins?

If you can manage to get me a contract with the public transport authority, I won't have to sell any more bacon.

I thought that given your political ideas, which are different from those of other rabbis, and your open mind, you'd understand.

Anyway, I have a million things to tell you that have nothing to do with pig farming, but I know you're busy, so I won't take up any more of your time and send you my deepest respect.

Harry Rosenmerck

# From Rabbi Moshe Cattan to Harry Rosenmerck
Nazareth, April 3, 2009

Mr. Rosenmerck,

Either you take me for an idiot or you are one. It could be both and you aren't aware of it. Do you see where I'm going with this?

Mr. Rosenmerck!

Come to my house. We can discuss the Talmud and I will restore the faith you seem to have replaced with commercial, ultracapitalist beliefs. For now, I'm responding to your letter point by point, but briefly, because Passover is coming soon and I have a lot to do.

1. If everyone reasoned the way you do, there would be no more morality. No more good or bad. The fact that someone else might sell bacon to that restaurant for degenerates, US Aviv, doesn't absolve you of the sin. If you were in a room with nine other men and a child who was starving to death, the fact that you ate the last piece of bread on the pretext that one of the nine others would have done it anyway does not excuse you: it would be you, YOU, who killed the child.

2.  It's been a long time since the poor Palestinians who blow themselves up on buses full of schoolchildren believed in anything at all, and even less so in the notion of virgins waiting for them. They're just trading their lives for a salary that will put a roof over their families' heads and guarantee they don't go hungry.

    You can keep your pig's blood. It would be better to take bricks out of the wall that separates us, and not so we can throw them in each other's faces, but rather to use them to build decent housing for the Palestinians.

3.  Israel doesn't give a damn about what the *New York Times* or anyone else thinks. We're the most hated country on Earth, sometimes justifiably, sometimes because that's just the way it is. We're not trying to please anyone or appear to be anyone other than who we are. Your pigs have an unparalleled stench and they are useless to the army.

I'll be expecting you at yeshiva. We'll talk.

Wash yourself in grace.

Yours sincerely,
Rabbi Moshe Cattan

## From David Rosenmerck to Harry Rosenmerck
Los Angeles, April 1, 2009

Dear Dad,

I keep writing despite your silence. To maintain a bond. So I won't one day find myself standing face-to-face with a stranger who'll turn out to be my father. So that I don't forget you.

Are you still mad? Because of that simple announcement? That simple phrase that changes my entire existence but not yours? Yes, I love men. Or "one man," I should say. I am in love, Dad. Don't you want to meet the person that makes your own son happy? Don't you want to talk to me and hear my laugh?

It's strange, the less I see you, the more I take after you. I look for you in my mirrors. I have your hair. The warmth of your hands in mine, even in winter. I surprise myself by wearing the turtlenecks I hated as a child and that you never went without when we lived in London. I have the same bald patch on my face that you can see now that I've grown a beard. I'm enclosing a photo.

I hope you're enjoying this strange adventure. To think that you refused to let me have a pet! Not even a goldfish! And now you're a breeder. Do you have anyone working for you? How many pigs do you have? Don't tell me it's you who takes care of them. Do you have boots and overalls? Mother tells me you don't have a phone, but I don't believe it. I wouldn't dare call you anyway. Silence hurts less on paper. We're all separated—Mother, Annabelle, you, and me. You're a piece of a puzzle on the wrong continent.

David

## From Monique Duchêne to Harry Rosenmerck
New York, April 2, 2009

Dear ex-husband who nevertheless remains the father of my children,

I'll be brief and to the point. You're a hopeless old schmuck. Your son has written you hundreds of letters and you haven't answered a single one.

If you could only see the success of his plays on their opening nights—applause that brings down the house. "A genius playwright," that was the headline in *La Repubblica* after the performance in Rome last week. But do you think he was smiling? No. Like every evening, he spent the whole performance watching the door instead of the stage, hoping he'd see you walk in.

Yell at him! Have an argument! Anything would be better than your cruel silence!

On the other hand, I want to thank you. I'm invited to all the New York dinners ever since you started breeding pigs. Every time I tell the story, it's a hit, although I'm not sure it's doing anything to reduce anti-Semitism!

Sniffer pigs for terrorists. Hahaha! And to think you got me to convert only for it to come to this.

Do you remember our first dinner over barbeque? How to pick up a goy?

Anyway, business is good. I've got new, interesting, and lucrative projects. Thank God for that, because with the alimony you give me . . .

Did I tell you that old goat Marina Duncan got remarried? To a Russian. Not a Jew. Just a Russian. And she had a face-lift. If she smiles, she's going to crack.

Any news from Annabelle? That's pretty. "News from Annabelle"—it could be the title of one of David's plays. She doesn't tell me anything. I think she's sad. She's in Paris, but she'll be coming back to New York as soon as she gets her damned degree. More than ten years of studying! She goes from an MBA to a doctorate—and for what? Just give us some grandchildren already!

Well, write to your son. His fiancé is charming, by the way. And get a telephone!

Monique

# From Harry Rosenmerck to Monique Duchêne
Nazareth, April 6, 2009

Dear Monique,

You call that brief? Your letter is two pages long and you drive me nuts.

Harry

# From Annabelle Rosenmerck to Harry Rosenmerck
Paris, April 10, 2009

Dear Daddy,

I know, long time, no hear—sorry. I was crying, crying my broken little heart out . . . It's hard to believe that tears evaporate and go to the same place as the water from the ocean, the rain, and the toilet bowl. I wish there were doctors for heartache. Not psychoanalysts or acupuncturists, no soft-science gurus. Real doctors who would localize the pain and disinfect it. It would sting painfully, but then it would be over. Then they'd cover it with a sort of paste—pink, like candy or marshmallows for toothless children—and the sadness would suffocate instead of me. And the wall would crack and his face would disappear, and mirrors would no longer reflect mine. And I'd pay the heartache doctor; I'd give him anything he asked. Then my lead shoes would stay there in front of the heartache doctor's office like an abandoned Dutch bicycle. The pink paste wouldn't erase the heartache—it isn't about getting rid of it—just turn it into nicer things like memories that make us laugh.

You're the only one I can talk to about my heartaches. Mom wants to be my friend and David is just too gay. Do you remember the first boy that hurt me? I was four. He liked Esmeralda better. I told him, "I love you, Didier. I want to be your girlfriend." He answered, "I like Esmeralda better." That seems to be the story of my life. And there's an Esmeralda hiding behind every door, just waiting to jump out like some kind of devil.

I went outside the school, without crying, and waited until none of the other kids could see me. Then I blew my nose on your shirt while I told you about my broken heart. You comforted me without saying much. I inhaled a sugared waffle and we sang in the car.

It's cold here. You'd think spring was never coming back. Maybe it's waiting for my smile, and I'm waiting for it.

I'm back to my old habits. I've been taking pictures all over the place, all the time. I'm enclosing a shot that's blurry, but I think there's a kind of magic to it. To me, this photo represents childhood.

How are the pigs? If you had a telephone, it'd be a lot easier, don't you think? If you die of swine flu (I know, totally random), who'll let me know?

Sending you kisses,
Your daughter,
Annabelle

## From Harry Rosenmerck to Rabbi Moshe Cattan
Nazareth, April 12, 2009

Dear Rabbi,

I can't come to your yeshiva. It's nothing personal, believe me. It's just that it took me a long time to get myself a color TV and now it's hard for me to see life in black-and-white.

They called me a dirty Jew back at school. I was five. I don't think my mother had mentioned that we were Jewish. I was a little boy—hers—but Jewish? I didn't know what that was. I wasn't circumcised so I wouldn't be identifiable without clothes. I was taught German so I could get by in the enemy's language and, secondarily, so I could read the philosophers in their original texts. Me, Jewish? Certainly. But obliged to subject myself to your ancestral fears and get caught up with your women in their wigs or your black cassocks and beards that sweat in the heat of the first days of spring? No thanks.

Nevertheless, thank you for the suggestion to wash. Breeding pigs doesn't make me one; on the other hand, your lack of sensitivity might make you one.

If you'd like to talk pigs or get me in a tefillin, you'll have to come to me. Or maybe we could meet for coffee in town?

When you make your life about religion, what do you know about life? Do you ever talk about feelings—anger, rage, love, or leaving God out of it?

I doubt it. How boring!

With all my respect, of course,
Harry Rosenmerck

From: david.rosenmerck@gmail.com
To: Annabelle.rosenmerck@mac.com
Date: April 12, 2009
Subject: From LAX heading to New York


Dear Sis,

You didn't get your blue-eyed lit professor to divorce? Who was right? How many tears did you cry? Enough to fill a glass or a bathtub? Did you put Band-Aids on your artichoke heart? My play is opening in New York next week and you will be there. That is final. It's a play about Dad, you know. Yes, I know, I've tried everything. Now I'm on to provocation. But I think it's my best writing yet. We're putting it on at The Flea, that little theatre where everything started for me. Do you remember when we bought all of the tickets for that opening night because we were terrified the actress would be playing to an empty room? And as a result, we filled it with Granny and her friends from bridge club (or bingo . . . I can't remember anymore— some kids' game)! Now people are fighting to get a seat. It's good to have *events* for the *happy few*. You see? I talk like a real fag now. But only in the emails I send to my sister, so don't worry. I would have sung you some Barbra Streisand over the phone but, as you may have noticed, you never answer.

Last week I was on a train (I live on planes and trains, where I write new plays that put me on more planes and trains). Two kids were sharing a sandwich and laughing hysterically. The smaller one was trying to eat the bigger one's portion and the latter was keeping guard with a fork, pretending that he wouldn't think twice about stabbing his sibling with it. You can't imagine how hard they were giggling.

Behind me, there was a little boy with his mother and he was devouring a sandwich all for him. Silently. His mother was reading.

I thought to myself: I was lucky to have had you, to pull on your pigtails and, later on, steal your dresses.

Things are happening in my life. I feel like you've missed twenty episodes from season five, and I thought I was your favorite series . . .

I need you, Annabelle.

Kisses,
David

## From Rabbi Moshe Cattan to Harry Rosenmerck
Nazareth, April 14, 2009

Dear Mr. Rosenmerck,

I see that I've offended you by asking you to wash yourself and, for that, I ask your forgiveness. I won't insist on having you come to the yeshiva so I can put you in your tefillin. As you know, our religion doesn't proselytize, and even less so to those who are already Jewish. (Are you really if you aren't circumcised? I'll have to ponder that question.)

Come and see me, Mr. Rosenmerck. I cannot come to you. It is forbidden for me to go anywhere near pigs.

Sincerely,
The Rabbi of Nazareth
Moshe Cattan

# From Harry Rosenmerck to Rabbi Moshe Cattan

Nazareth, April 16, 2009

Dear Sir Rabbi,

I'm sorry to hear that a tiny piece of skin hidden in my underwear might prevent me from being one of the chosen people. You know, I'm a nice guy even if I do like ham. Sacrilege!

Did you know that you're going to be a celebrity to the young, trendy generation of Tel Aviv? That letter full of insults you sent to the US Aviv restaurant has been laminated and is being used for place mats. And on the menu next to the eggs and bacon, it says, "This dish has been recommended by Rabbi Moshe Cattan."

Because stories transform over time, maybe someday they'll call the dish "Cattan Eggs"?

One last thing: why in the hell should I have to come to you?

With all my respect,
Harry Rosenmerck

# From Annabelle Rosenmerck to David Rosenmerck
Paris, April 18, 2009

My dearest David,

There's something I've never been able to tell you about and it's haunting me.

What were you doing on September 11th? You remember, of course. Everyone remembers. Everyone experienced it in their own way. One thought it was an action movie, another had a cousin in the tower, this one was at home, frozen and speechless.

And me. What about me, David?

Remember how all three of you tried calling me to no avail until Mom was crying and screaming to the point of making herself sick?

I was probably climaxing when the towers fell. Getting my jollies under the body of a married man forty years my senior. The world was discovering that it was mortal as a whole, and me, how bizarre aging cocks looked encircled by white pubic hair. That was the first time. He spent months convincing me. Not to sleep with him, but to betray his wife. I'd run into her several times. She was a professor, too. A pretty, dry woman with piercing blue eyes. It was like she could read everything in us. She looked so straight, terribly moral. She gave me the chills. He was the one cheating on her, but it was my morality I was cutting a notch in.

September 11th. We spent the whole day in the sack. We'd used a long conference in New York as an excuse. Our loved ones kept trying to reach us in vain. He admitted to me later that he'd used Viagra. He was like a teenager craving my body, or a vampire sucking all of my youth while I thought he was giving me strength.

We were careless and we came out guilty. It was the room service waiter who told us. It must have been about 7 p.m. He came to the door trembling and dropped the plate of spaghetti Bolognese that Andrew had ordered. "Sorry, it's the news." "What news?" And the little waiter turned on the television. I was coming out of the bathroom wearing a bathrobe, and the towers came crashing down on my convictions.

I didn't have a cell phone back then. While Andrew listened to the dozens of messages from his wife and children, I was frantically dialing your number. You were all together—Dad, Mom, and you—when I told you I was fine, and you started crying.

It's strange how human beings confuse the world's stories with their own. How megalomaniacal we are, even in moments of horror. I felt responsible for the towers. As if my decadence, my cries of pleasure drowned out those of the people who were falling to the pavement. My breasts on the chest of a married man—as if all of that were part of the disaster.

So I thought to myself, "I'm in love with Andrew." Without that, I'd have thought of myself as dirty and disgusting. I needed to transform my day of discovery and selfishness into a day of love. And I've dragged this guilt around for all these years.

I never went back to Boston University. I enrolled at NYU. Andrew brought me my bag the following week and came to see me regularly. I was like a woman trapped in a whorehouse. Utterly defeated. Unable to leave New York, trapped in that guilt. I started a new thesis, "The Chaos Theory and Monotheistic Religions."

Whenever I pulled away and then returned to him, Professor Andrew Black thought he was getting me back with his charm; but it was the towers that kept falling in my heart.

Annabelle

# From Rabbi Moshe Cattan to Harry Rosenmerck
Nazareth, April 20, 2009

Dear Mr. Rosenmerck,

Come and see me for several reasons. First, your livestock is in danger. I am very involved in the social, religious, and political life of Nazareth. Believe me, you're upsetting people. Also, I do have occasion to talk about things other than religion. Movies, for example. And cooking! (What a pleasure to appear on the menu of a restaurant with a cynical owner! My lawyer will take care of that.) I am a real gourmet and inherited numerous Tunisian recipes from my mother. Are you familiar with this cuisine? Made with olive oil, I'll give you, but unequaled. Come for Passover and eat a *bkeila*! And let us end these tense exchanges. I am curious to see your face, Mr. Rosenmerck; but if you insist, I am capable of filling an entire notebook with insults in multiple languages.

Sincerely, of course,
The Rabbi of Nazareth
Moshe Cattan

From: moniqueduchene@yahoo.com
To: Annabelle.rosenmerck@mac.com
Date: April 21, 2009
Subject: From your mother

Dear Annabelle,

Your brother told me about your relationship being over. I knew long distance wouldn't work. I won't say I told you so because you already know that.

It's for the best. You two never had a future.

When are you going to start working? You'll be fulfilled and you'll meet a man who deserves you.

You're not just going to collect master's degrees and MBAs! In the meantime, your breasts will fall and your belly will get soft! You're so beautiful. That would be such a shame.

I'll stop being a nagging mother now, but I want so much for you to be happy. I suppose that's an idle dream.

Everything plays out in childhood. You're looking for your father because he left us for the first two years of your life. Some wounds never heal—they're the ones that kill us. We stubbornly allow ourselves to be stabbed again and again in the same place. Once we localize the wound that will never scar over, we spend our lives reopening it. But sometimes, a twist of fate transforms everything. Or you meet a man whose neurosis covers up your wound and it works.

That's how it worked for a long time between your father and me. Me, a girl from Lille raised by nuns—I found a foolproof way to drive my parents nuts. Then, they stopped being anti-Semitic and started liking your father, and I stopped.

I don't know what to tell you, my little Annabelle. Go see your father; he always knew how to comfort you better than I did.

Mom

# From David Rosenmerck to Annabelle Rosenmerck
New York, April 25, 2009

Annabelle,

On September 11th, when the first tower fell, I was listening to the radio in a taxi on the way to a meeting with a movie producer who wanted me to adapt *Who Am I?* into a movie. They still thought it was an accident when I walked into his office. I called you right away and there was that stupid song from the musical on your answering machine.

"Did you see it?" I asked, and waited for you to answer. I said, "Annabelle," and your name echoed in your empty room. I continued my interview like a robot. The television was on behind the producer and I saw the second plane fly into the tower. I was trying to explain to this fat, bald guy that something was happening behind him that warranted our stopping all discussion, but he said, "We'll deal with that afterward."

He wanted to talk about himself. He had a cigarette that he sucked on between snippets of meaningless dialogue. So I left. Without explaining. Without answering. The guy insulted me when I got to the end of the hall. I went right to Mom's. Dad was already there, as if together they could be stronger in order to protect you.

The three of us stayed together until eleven o'clock that night, waiting for a sign from you. Mom was trying to find out where that famous conference could be happening. She's the one who paid for your ticket from Boston to New York. Your roommate at BU was positive: you had left for New York the night before.

And I thought that, if you died, Dad would certainly forgive me and there'd be something simpler in my life.

And yet, Annabelle, you know how much I love you. But I couldn't unthink that thought, which came from a part of myself that I hate.

You see, we all have our dark sides. We're working it out in these letters and we'll get rid of them.

David

# From Harry Rosenmerck to Rabbi Moshe Cattan
Nazareth, April 26, 2009

Dear Mister Rabbi,

I went into the center of Nazareth yesterday to meet my old friend Hassan and we stayed to smoke some *shisha*.

Otherwise, I think I'd have come to see you so we could have a laugh and taste your *"bkeila"* made with olive oil! What is it, anyway? I don't even know how to pronounce it.

Since I'm not coming to you, I'll make you laugh by correspondence and I'll be none the wiser. If you laugh in an empty forest, does it make a sound?

Have you seen that new travel agency run by one of your sinister colleagues? It's called "Memorial Tours."

These tours aren't concerts with Chabads dressed up like the Beatles or Michael Jackson—they're organized trips to the high temples of suffering that are Poland, Germany, Austria, and the former Czechoslovakia. There is a 3-day, Auschwitz-Birkenau/ Theresienstadt itinerary by bus. Or a more luxurious itinerary that lets you take the time to cry, with outings to four concentration camps in three days, then a discovery weekend in

Prague with visits to the old synagogue and Kafka's house. The kosher meals are included.

Woody Allen could just set up his camera in front of the place and start rolling.

The worst is that this guy is totally oblivious to the vulgarity of his agency. He even pushed one of these Prozac trips on a couple of guilt-ridden goys—or goys made to feel guilty for the occasion—right in front of me. I can just see the sun hats he could offer with his vacation packages:

"I've been to Auschwitz."

Auschtrip

Summer concentration camp

Shoadventures

Or, more intellectual, Birkenolodge

Frankly, Mr. Rabbi, instead of spending your days trying to make me feel guilty over a few strips of bacon, you should put an end to these antics.

Plus, after consulting with my lawyer—Mr. Buchman—I can confirm that Nazareth is a city apart. The law of 1962 forbidding pig breeding in Israel and authorizing their slaughter is not valid in certain Arab villages, which are mentioned in the law, due to their denser Christian populations—like Kfar-Yasif, Ibillin, Galilee, and . . . Nazareth.

So your threats only interest me as a basis for correspondence to which I've grown attached; you can't do anything to my little pink animals.

You'll most likely receive this letter on the morning of Shabbat and so I wish you a peaceful one.

Your friend,
Harry Rosenmerck

From: Annabelle.rosenmerck@mac.com
To: moniqueduchene@yahoo.com
Date: April 27, 2009
Subject: From your daughter


Dear Mom,

I've been in therapy for seven years, thank you. You've told me many times how my father's departure and subsequent return traumatized me.

I'm astonished that you didn't remind me for the hundredth time about the Freudian episode when I shit in my shoes to celebrate our reunion.

And, of course, what a caricature: I slept with an "old" professor the same age as Dad.

What really bothers you is that, like a lot of "stupid tarts" my age, I've come to hunt in your territory, to eat from your plate. So you think, "Serves her right" if he patches things up with his wife in rollers and you never, never think I might be grieving.

Yes, stop analyzing everything. I'm grieving.

I don't give a shit about which neuroses made you love Dad and then stop. I'd like to feel love when you talk to me, but it's pointless.

Annabelle

# From Harry Rosenmerck to Annabelle Rosenmerck
Nazareth, April 26, 2009

My dearest daughter,

Thank you for the little piece of childhood that you sent me. Take pictures, don't stop. Sometimes we see things more clearly when we're not in front of them. And that camera that seems so cold is bringing you closer to life.

How I envy you the winter that's hanging on. Here, there's no fresh air.

And yet it'll snow in Israel in a few months and the sun will be over Paris in a week.

The same is true of heartbreak. And that's what makes it sad, more so than the end of love—that it passes. That everything goes away. That everything escapes.

If I had a telephone, we'd never say anything to each other. Nothing important.

I don't have any pink paste like the heartache doctor, but there's a little piglet I'm bottle-feeding that would make you feel better. I can't offer you waffles either, but there's a *bomboloni* seller around the corner—you know, those big Tunisian doughnuts they fry in boiling oil and then dust with sugar.

Come to me. We'll sing in the car. I've lost an octave, but I still have rhythm. I'll introduce you to my friends: Marc, an enlightened English Christian, Josef, a rabbi who wants to play rock, and Hassan, the richest of us all, gardener to the Nazareth bourgeoisie and a Muslim who smokes weed.

You see, all of our dinners start like a joke and we just wait for the punch line.

See you very soon, my little girl,
Your dad

p.s. Stop picking the same kind of man. Learn to love the ones that love you. Get married, have kids, and get fat like everybody else.

From: moniqueduchene@yahoo.com
To: Annabelle.rosenmerck@mac.com
Date: April 27, 2009
Subject: Sorry

My beloved daughter,

Forgive me, it was clumsy of me to ask you to stop studying so you could fall in love. When you were a little girl, I always put your intelligence ahead of your heart, and now I think that might have been a mistake. I've always had the impression that we speak different languages. Come home so I can take you in my arms—that would be simpler.

And no, absolutely not, I don't go after men in their sixties anymore. I'm focusing all my efforts on rich ones in their eighties with heart conditions so it'll be brief but intense—and I'll inherit!

When I hit the jackpot, you should come to NYC and we'll waste an entire morning shopping before going to eat at Katz's. You love those giant pastrami sandwiches and all the photos of Woody Allen (or is it Mel Brooks . . . ?).

Mom

# From Harry Rosenmerck to Rabbi Moshe Cattan
Nazareth, April 30, 2009

Dear Mr. Rabbi,

I got your letter forbidding me from making any jokes about the Shoah.

My parents were at Birkenau. That's where I was conceived.

I never asked how.

I'm living proof that we make love with bones more than flesh.

My mother survived. I was the only thing she had left of my father. She left with a tiny bulge in her belly and I held on tightly to her insides. I was born in Paris three months after the liberation. My mother started a new life with a baby and a sense of humor. Back then, she wrote comedies that actors read on the radio. She would have found the idea of me raising pigs in Nazareth hysterical! The laughter would have killed her if cancer hadn't already done the job three years ago. I took her body to Herzliya Cemetery and stayed with her.

I'll tell you what I think. I think that Israel was created because of, or thanks to, that horror we now call the Shoah. So that there could be a place, just one, where no one would tell Jews they didn't belong. So we wouldn't die by the thousands because we have a particular name or are missing a piece of foreskin. I think that if you allow jokes about it, then the Shoah will gradually slip away into the pain of history. And when this atrocity is part of history, then you won't be able to tolerate certain actions taken in the name of Israel. No more walls. No more meaning to the Jewish State. No more pigs on stilts? No more Palestinians humiliated at the border. No more deprivation for our neighbors while our youth gorge themselves. No more rifles in the backs of the majority. No more religions on our passports. No more reasons for our children to risk their lives because they have the misfortune of getting on the wrong bus to go to school in the wrong country. No more justification for the absurdity of our lives and our situation. I'm telling you, Mr. Rabbi, if we'd only make a few jokes about the Shoah, nobody would wait for Godot anymore. Would that be so bad? I don't know. It has to happen. Does keeping the memory fresh prevent history from repeating itself? Surely not. Memories are meant to be forgotten. History is meant to be repeated. That of Jews, of women, of Arabs, of people who suffer, of Little Red Riding Hood. And the grandmother always, always has sharp teeth.

Dr. Harry Rosenmerck

From: david.rosenmerck@gmail.com
To: moniqueduchene@yahoo.com
Date: May 1, 2009
Subject: Your son is rich!


Mom,

I know you mean well by sending me these little cash transfers for every Jewish holiday. But a wire transfer for Passover? First of all, it was last month!

Go see a shrink! You don't need to pay to prove to me that you're Jewish. Even if Dad's family always considered you a convert, I've always considered you my mother.

Religion doesn't mean much to me. Of course, it's the cradle of civilization and it has a certain place in my writing. The Jewish religion brings out the best and worst of humanity. And I don't *feel* Jewish; I *am* Jewish, you see? The two things are very different.

I'm pale, I wear glasses, I'm homosexual, I'm small, and I'm Jewish. I endure. I'm doing something with it. The beatings I took at school, more for being Jewish than small and cross-eyed, I now transform into words. To try to understand. Judaism is an exclusive club. A non-proselytizing religion. Now there's a concept. "We're not going to spend insane amounts of money to evangelize, send boats, and kill recalci-trant natives—no, let's be elitist!"

Membership card: no foreskin. Must have a Jewish mother, terrible taste in food, etc.

And we're shocked that those on the outside question the actions of this very private club, reputed for its sense of humor and money (what an incredible marketing coup—ninety percent are deprived of both), and cannot understand why, on top of that, they shouldn't hate us.

To sum it up, Mother, don't bother paying your membership dues for Passover. I'm not the treasurer. And I earn an indecent amount of money on the pretext that I put words into an amusing order. Give double to Annabelle, buy yourself some dresses, or get your breasts redone.

Love,
David

p.s. I can't have dinner with you Tuesday. I'm going to the home of a publisher whose highly perceptive wife is taken with me.

From: Annabelle.rosenmerck@mac.com
To: david.rosenmerck@gmail.com
Date: May 2, 2009
Subject: Departure . . .

My dear David,

I'm writing to you from the airport in Paris. I'm really sorry but my research is taking me to Montana, so I'll have to miss your play . . . once again . . .

When are you coming to visit me in Paris?

I miss you and want to see your fiancé. I've only met him once. I was drunk (or was he?). And anyway that didn't count; I thought it was just a one-night stand . . .

It makes me sick to know I can't be there tomorrow. Really . . .

Love,
Your sister

From: david.rosenmerck@gmail.com
To: Annabelle.rosenmerck@mac.com
Date: May 2, 2009
Subject: Pure of heart

Young lady,

I could get angry and hope for your plane to be hijacked by an alter-globalist armed with a biodegradable knife and the intention to crash it into a field of transgenic corn.

You're all terrible liars . . .

Even in writing.

See you tomorrow in New York,
David

# From Annabelle Rosenmerck to Harry Rosenmerck
New York, May 3, 2009

Dear Dad,

I'm at the café across the street from The Flea. I took a plane this morning. David doesn't know . . . well, I'm not sure . . . I think he might have found me out. We'll see! I'm waiting for David's play to open and I'm three hours early. It's being put on in the same theatre where he started. At his request! What a snob, right? Now that he's filling theatres that seat a thousand, he's going back to limited seating. I guess he's trying to find that high he got from *Who Am I?* The reality is that he's still brilliant, but a lot less so since he's said that he is. As if that millstone hanging around his neck containing his secret also enclosed painful treasures of inspiration. I think that was the last time we were together as a family. There was Granny's funeral, too, but even if we all four went, we weren't together at that point. I get the impression Mom gets a certain pleasure out of tension. She likes stories, problems, having the right to criticize. And then she'll manage to be the only girl in her son's life . . . By the way, from listening to her, you'd think I wasn't her type. Never enough makeup. Unkempt fingernails. "Poorly groomed," that's her famous expression. "Annabelle, you are poorly groomed . . ." Or she'll moan, "It's such a shame . . ." Anyway, she's split us into two couples—she and David being one, and the two of us the other, the sort of embarrassing couple that she has to see from time to time. I saw my shrink before getting on the plane, so you're getting my forty minutes of rumination . . . for free! In any case, I'm here because I don't want her to get away with it, and because I miss my brother.

It must be so hard, Dad! All these years of silence. They'll never come back. And time just keeps dying. David is the same. He doesn't wear pink skirts or giggle with a falsetto voice. He's the little boy you raised—as stubborn as ever, and as handsome and strong. Also, as tormented by justice and truth. Also, impatient. You're smiling as you read this, right? I know you're dreaming of seeing him but just don't know how to go about it anymore. One word from you and I'll bring him with me.

I'll be in Israel next week. It's time I met the new you. I won't lie to you—nobody thinks this pig farming will last. I think you've just been fooling all of us for the past two years and sending us fake pictures!

There's also the fact that I need to know where my life really is. In New York, where I studied, where I became a woman, where I have friends? In London, where we were born? In France, where Mom is from? I thought I'd settle in New York, but David is never around and Mom would want a spare set of my keys! Maybe there, in Israel? When I'm far away, it's my homeland, but as soon as I spend a day there, I feel like a foreigner among those people. All of the Israelis carry such internal strength, but also violence, and coarseness—almost vulgarity. I don't think the fact that they're at war justifies all of that . . . You're going to tell me that we can't generalize; but I believe, quite to the contrary, that a mixture of places and people creates either good or bad energy that then defines the atmosphere of a country. In fact, I haven't found my own country yet.

Maybe it was in that café, where all four of us used to have breakfast on Sundays; maybe that was my country? The country of childhood that I don't want to let go.

I can see David walking up the street. He's flipped the collar of his long black coat and keeps his eyes to the ground. I'm folding this letter and mailing it—otherwise, it'll never end.

I love you, Dad,
Annabelle

p.s. It's a nightmare not being able to call you. I'll figure out how to get you my flight times ASAP!

# From Rabbi Moshe Cattan to Harry Rosenmerck
Nazareth, May 4, 2009

Dear Harry,

I'm taking the liberty of calling you by your first name, and you can call me Moshe.

I don't know anything about you. Let's start over from the beginning, shall we? Why did your anger, or pride, make you sign your last letter "Dr."? What did you do before? Are you married? Do you have any children? How or why do you feel Jewish? I mean if it isn't the practice of religion or faith that makes you Jewish . . . could it be the horror your parents were put through?

I didn't suffer from that, you see. I suffered the violence a posteriori. More as a human being than a Jew. I wasn't yet born. I'm a young rabbi. I'm thirty-nine years old. I've met numerous survivors and something that has gone out in their eyes has lit something in my heart that forbids any jokes about horror. It can only be spoken of as a historical fact. Because if we have the right to deform a reality in order to make it amusing, then someday we'll be able to change it to make it a gaping hole, empty, nonexistent. And on that day, neither Israel nor anyone will protect us.

Being a rabbi doesn't prevent me from having honed a personal political opinion. I don't systematically agree with Israel, nor do I always disagree.

My son will be eighteen next month. He doesn't want to be religious. He's going to go into the army, because he doesn't have a choice. He tells me there are choices other than God or war. Not here. Here, it's God or war and each lives for the other.

Do you think I enjoy that? Do you know what it's like to tremble as your children leave for school, just because they're climbing onto a bus? Can you manage to avoid thinking about death always lurking?

I'm expecting you and your family for Shabbat. My address is on the back of the envelope. If you can't make it on foot because I live too far away, then I'll expect you on Sunday. If you can't make it Sunday, then come on Monday.

People live next door to each other and never speak to each other. Have you ever observed a city from the window of an airplane? We're just little ants, convinced of our own importance, of being the hero of the story. None of it makes any sense unless we meet one another and share. I'm eager to know you. Forgive me if I hurt you.

Sincerely,
Moshe

# From David Rosenmerck to Harry Rosenmerck
New York, May 4, 2009

Dear Dad,

Yesterday was the opening of my play. We were all together. Mom looked like a Christmas tree—the older she gets, the more jewelry she wears. Every time she laughed, it sounded like sleigh bells. Annabelle surprised me by showing up. I invited her, like I always do, but I didn't really think she'd come. A little pale, but so sweet. She's too kind to be happy. Any normal person would crush her to bits. It's not that they want to hurt her, no . . . She's like a ladybug; we pass it from one finger to another to spread happiness and we clumsily tear off a leg, then a wing, and then we crush it.

And you were there too, Dad, as played by Robert Etrica (I know you've always hated him, which amuses me even more). The play is called *Kosher Pig*. I could have come up with a more sophisticated title, I know. But it sells. By the way, it's already being translated in several countries, including Israel. I'll be there in a few months. Is that enough to make you watch *The Birdcage* or *Eyes Wide Open*? For you to reread Oscar Wilde? For you to go into therapy? For you to cry for the grandchildren you'll never have from me? (The ladybug can take care of that, on the other hand.) And for you to talk to me—even if you want to yell or cry? I'm counting on seeing you before you die, or before I do.

I'm changing. I'm getting older. I still have all my hair; it's very dark. On the other hand, my beard is going white. I wear even thicker glasses now. My vision's not getting any better. Apparently, this makes me charming. No doubt: when you're successful, everything makes you charming. Unemployed with trifocals—not so much. I'm going to end up going blind. All the better since, with age, I imagine you have to be less demanding in terms of your visual choices. I'll find everyone attractive. I like to hear things before I see them. When I heard Lawrence's footstep, I knew I loved him. And I waited for him to love me back.

What about your love life? Do you have a girlfriend? Do you get laid? Have you rekindled an old flame? Do you feel any love, at least?

I ask you these questions mostly so you'll ask them of yourself. So you'll be happy. Because you don't answer me.

I have the terrifying impression that I've never been closer to you than since you went silent.

I don't know what your voice sounds like now. I have a memory of the one that read me stories when I was a little boy. The voice of *Zeralda's Ogre*. You must have been the age that I am now.

David

## From Annabelle Rosenmerck to Harry Rosenmerck
New York, May 4, 2009

Dad,

I'm still in shock from David's play. It was incredible. You'll probably take it the wrong way, but God, what a declaration of love for you! It's so unfair that even in family relationships, we love the ones that hurt us.

To think I said that he'd lost his inspiration—well, you might say that your absence has given him a different kind. It's unsettling to go and see your brother's shows, to get close to the mechanisms and inner workings of the whole thing—closer, even, than he does, it seems, since he only writes by instinct—and, most of all, to know he is one of the most important writers of our time.

We celebrated his thirty-fifth yesterday. There were about twenty of us. All our old friends were there—some came with their young spouses. The Soussans' son, fat Delphine, the "rat," who's now a trader and married to a pretty Belgian! Josephine, David's first girlfriend—still a knockout and single . . . anyway, it was fun.

David gave a little speech in which he wanted to say something nice about you, but I saw that his smile was really a smirk to hold back tears.

Like that face he used to make, so angry, when we were kids.

I don't know how you manage to do without him. You should at least get on a plane and come see the play without telling anyone.

I haven't gotten my ticket for Tel Aviv yet, but I couldn't wait to tell you all of that. And to tell you that Mom was so proud. Does that surprise you? You managed to turn a shy Catholic girl from Lille into a tacky Sephardic Jew—quite an accomplishment for an autistic Ashkenazi. You'd think that inside every woman there's a Jew just waiting to come out.

I'm just waiting to find the man who'll make me a mother.

I love you, dearest Daddy.

We'll finally be together soon,
Annabelle

## From Monique Duchêne to Harry Rosenmerck
New York, May 4, 2009

Harry,

You missed the premiere of David's play yesterday. It was sublime. And it was wonderful to have kids who love you and are proud to have you as a mother . . . You, on the other hand, you're getting a really bad rap.

Annabelle has gotten so thin. She's heartbroken and I don't know what to say to her.

Think about sending a simple card to your son for his birthday. He misses you.

Monique

# From Harry Rosenmerck to Rabbi Moshe Cattan
Nazareth, May 8, 2009

Dear Moshe,

Thank you for the dinner we had together. I really enjoyed the *bkeila*. When you set it down on the table, I thought I was going to be sick, but I ended up eating every bite. It's as delicious as it is ugly! How do you make it? I guess it's a secret recipe! Otherwise, I'd try to make some for my daughter, who gets in next week. Now I know why the Sephardim are fat and have no sense of humor. We Ashkenazi have to compensate and laugh while eating stuffed carp—anything to avoid thinking about what we're eating! You simply enjoy it.

It's strange—given your open mind, I'd have thought the women would have mixed with us. Those two tables—you have a lot in common with Muslims after all.

In any case, your wife sure speaks her mind. I liked that a lot. My ex-wife was like that: the kind of ballbuster you can be proud of. Sorry, but it's sort of true.

Thank her.

See you soon,
Harry

# From Rabbi Moshe Cattan to Harry Rosenmerck
Nazareth, May 10, 2009

Dear Harry,

I hope I get the chance to meet your daughter. My family was pleased to have you here. My wife found you "pretentious," but nice! I won't dwell on the comparison with your ex-"ballbuster." We had a lovely evening. Following is my mother's recipe for *bkeila* (everyone called her Nana—*minth*, in Arabic—because she made a memorable mint tea). I hope you appreciate the significance of this act of friendship.

*Place 1.5 kilos of spinach in a bowl, wash, mince, and fry in a large stew pot. As soon as the leaves begin to brown, begin stirring, over and over, so they continue to brown without burning. When they're dark and crunchy, pour in 2 liters of water. Add a large onion, cubed, three small garlic cloves, peeled and chopped, then 250g of white beans. Then, add the spices: a dozen fresh mint leaves, finely chopped, two spoons of ground cinnamon, salt, and pepper.*

*When the ingredients start to bind and the mixture begins to boil, add the meat (kosher, of course!)—an ox foot and two pounds of duck. Sometimes, I add in some veal...*

*Serve piping hot and enjoy!*

You'll see, it's easy to find the Ashkenazi sense of humor two or three days after digestion.

Sincerely,
Moshe

From: Annabelle.rosenmerck@mac.com
To: david.rosenmerck@gmail.com
Date: May 10, 2009
Subject: Don't tell (Aviv)


Dear David,

I bitched for two hours because Dad wasn't there to pick me up at the Tel Aviv airport. Then I found my letter giving him my arrival times at the bottom of my purse. Oops!

I forgot to mail it. I had no telephone, just an address. My God, I felt so free! Me, the thirty-three-year-old student . . . with no schedule, no commitments, no man. I lit a cigarette. Then I rented a car and decided to take my time heading toward his place. That was yesterday. And I'm realizing that I'm heading toward myself.

Tel Aviv has changed so much. You'll see. The young people are beautiful, free, straightforward, and aggressive. Men kiss each other in the middle of the street. You see soldiers alongside tall blondes in leggings, Falashas baked in foil (it isn't a local specialty, but the devout Ethiopian Jews!), and gorgeous guys with piercings.

It's the new swinging London, with sunshine thrown in for free. I got a hotel room with the intention of going to Dad's the next day. Then I went out for a walk.

I felt pretty. I've lost a lot of weight thanks to my fucking broken heart. I was wearing a little white dress over my pale freckled skin, hiding behind my camera lens, like I always do, peeking out from behind it to see what I could shoot.

Then, this guy looked me straight in the eyes and said something in Hebrew. I said I didn't speak his language and he said, without missing a beat, "I like you. Come."

He took my hand and I gestured that I hadn't yet paid, so he threw a twenty-shekel bill on the table and pulled me with him. It was three o'clock in the afternoon and the sun was blazing overhead. My hand started to get clammy in his, which was dry and rough. I was just starting to get a closer look at him—he had a sort of animal quality about him that exceeded his beauty, but he was seductive: tall, dark-haired with green eyes.

I said, "Annabelle."

Then I repeated my name so he'd tell me his: "Avi."

We crossed a few streets and then walked up some stairs into a building. I thought he was taking me to his place. I wasn't thinking at all, actually. I was trying to keep my heart from exploding out of my chest.

It was a dark apartment—all the shutters were closed. It looked like a nightclub in the middle of the day. Not a teen dance party, more like a sulfurous lair. There were people dancing, drinking, and kissing each other on the mouth. So we did all three. Then, he took me into an even darker corner of the apartment. He pulled up my dress and we made love. People walked past us from time to time but no one seemed bothered. A song came on and people sang along—their shouts masked mine when I came. You can't imagine how beautiful Avi was, how he held on to me firmly with his hands. For a brief moment, I felt tiny and protected. I felt beautiful. Afterward, we went back out into the street and smiled at each other for a long time. He gave me one last kiss on the lips and, before turning to leave, made a movement that invited me to follow. I looked down for a second and by the time I looked back up, he was already far away, just a back in the crowd. I barely had the time to grab my camera.

Annabelle

# From Harry Rosenmerck to Monique Duchêne
Nazareth, May 11, 2009

Dear Monique,

I don't know where to send letters to Annabelle and her mobile isn't working. She was supposed to arrive two days ago, but I never received her flight times.

You're not answering your phone either. I hope everything is OK.

I'm heading back into town today to try and get in touch with her. You can leave me a message in a café I usually go to in Nazareth. The number is 00 972 345 2612.

Thanks for not leaving me in the dark.

Harry

# From Monique Duchêne to Harry Rosenmerck
New York, May 14, 2009

Harry,

I left a message at the café. The owner isn't exactly charming. Since I'm not sure he'll pass along the message, I'm repeating in this letter that Annabelle is fine. She sent an email to her brother. She's taking a little tour before coming to your place in a rental car. By the time you read this, her little face probably will have walked through the door of your pigpen.

This fear, this anguish over not hearing from someone you love, I know it well!

Do you remember? Two years before we separated, you left for a week without giving me any explanation. You just said that you needed it. And I told myself that if you were going to cheat on me, you'd have found a better excuse, a real pretext. So I believed you. What did you do during that week? Can you tell me now that there's a statute of limitations? It would do me some good.

Love,
Monique

From: david.rosenmerck@gmail.com
To: Annabelle.rosenmerck@mac.com
Date: May 14, 2009
Subject: Rosy cheeks


My dear sister,

The fact that I am homosexual doesn't make me your girlfriend. I am still your big brother and, frankly, I don't want to hear about how you got banged by some big tan guy.

Having said that, I'm very jealous.

It's good to feel alive. I remember when you were little and all pale. You never ran around outside. Mom smothered us like a hen does its eggs. You read everything you could get your hands on. I must have started writing in the hopes of finding a reader like you. I rebelled—I went out to play soccer so I could look at my friends' butts. But you were pallid. It only took two minutes of jogging for you to be out of breath and rosy-cheeked. That must be how you looked when you said goodbye to Avi.

Are you at Dad's yet? I can't believe he's a pig farmer. It's bizarre to me. He doesn't talk to me anymore and doesn't answer my letters. I feel like a kid somebody made up an incredible story for so they didn't have to tell me my father is dead. Send me proof of life!

It's pretty quiet here. The telephone doesn't ring as much. The reviews were horrible. It was bound to happen . . . They destroy what they create. I was a big ball of yarn and now they're pulling the string in the other direction . . . When I'm no more than a piece of string full of knots, they'll wind me back into a nice ball again. Or not . . .

Who cares! I'm enclosing one of the reviews—lethal, but so well written. I want to seduce the journalist. Yes, a strange turn-on, I admit. Go outside, live! I want to meet you in Tel Aviv, in Paris, or somewhere else, with rosy cheeks.

Your brother,
David

# Kosher Pork
by Zach Frederick

Last night, I attended the New York premiere of the latest play by the young but nevertheless dramatic writer David Rosenmerck. The feigned conviviality of happy friends spoiled by fate surrounded the few journalists who were hand-picked to assess the work.

Far from relaxing me, the conviviality stained me. One of those greasy, thick stains that you can never get out. One would have thought that the members of the audience had made a preshow pact to laugh and cry over the fate of the play's hero, played by Robert Etrica encased in jeans so tight he couldn't walk. Perhaps he was given electric shocks at the appropriate moments, because for me, there was no joy, no pain—except for the future of American theater—and having not received advance notice, I didn't know when to laugh.

As for Etrica, perhaps he is right for this role after all. Rosenmerck, whose directorial debut will be his death sentence, thought it best to have him perform with his back turned almost entirely to the audience.

From: moniqueduchene@yahoo.com
To: Annabelle.rosenmerck@mac.com
Date: May 14, 2009
Subject: The Jewish mother is coming out


Annabelle,

This brief email is to tell you that your father is worried and also because we didn't really get a chance to talk while you were in New York. We've never really gotten a chance to talk. I don't know where to start with you. You intimidated me even when you were little. You seemed to know everything better than I did. And I truly believe that to be the case.

Perhaps we won't get a chance to talk, but I would like to tell you things: that I love you, that I'm proud of you, and that I hope to see you in love. Enjoy your father.

I love you very much,
Mom

From: Annabelle.rosenmerck@mac.com
To: moniqueduchene@yahoo.com
Date: May 16, 2009
Subject: Re: The Jewish mother is coming out


Mom,

Are you sick and hiding it from me or is this just menopause?

We don't have to talk for me to know that you love me. That you love me too much. That your love smothered us—me and David—to the point of not needing to love anybody else.

I'm not going to Dad's until tomorrow.

I don't check my emails every day. I've been captured by Tel Aviv and the country I've been running from for years. What wealth! What creativity! And the people are so beautiful. All of the different combinations. That's what is astonishing here—the interbreeding. The opposite of what you would expect. There is nothing monotheistic about this place, and the look of the soldiers doesn't make you want to be monogamous either.

Still, I dream of making you happy and falling in love. How does that happen, Mom? And what if it never happens to me? I'm talking about those reciprocal, healthy loves. The ones you see in well-lit advertisements. That exists, doesn't it? All the men I ever loved were either unavailable or didn't love me back. The only thing I've gotten from love is burned.

I love you, too,
Annabelle, who knows everything

# From Rabbi Moshe Cattan to Harry Rosenmerck
Nazareth, May 17, 2009

My dear Harry,

Most people agree that the prohibition of pork in religions, and in ours in particular, has to do with the question of hygiene. But I have another theory. Pigs are a lot like us. When that plane crashed in the Andes and the survivors had to feed on the cadavers of their fellow passengers to survive, they said that they tasted exactly like pork. I imagine you've seen quite a few piglets on your farm. Have you noticed how closely they resemble our own babies? There's something troubling about that. I don't think we should eat an animal that eats its own feces, trash, anything—including its own kind—so that we don't end up like it. So that we can preserve what we call our "humanity."

Western societies have done the same thing with dogs and cats, but no one seems to be conscious of the fact that it's the same kind of prohibition! In the collective subconscious, not eating pork often symbolizes being Jewish. We don't eat shrimp, horse, or snails, either, and we don't turn on lights on Saturday. But what most often defines us is the exclusion of pork from our diets. Incidentally, I say the word "pork" rather a lot for a rabbi— most of us don't even put it in writing. To avoid naming it in the Talmud, we say "*davar acher*," which means something else, "another thing."

Despite the long list of things forbidden to Jews in Deuter-onomy, Christians had forgotten about everything but *davar acher* by the Middle Ages. They wrote stories in which Jews ate pork and were executed for it. Even worse, the medieval anti-Semites used pork, little by little, to symbolize Jews. Sometimes it was an illustration of Jewish children suckling a sow, or eating its shit. And that continued right up to the Nazi propaganda. It was a heinous charge: "You don't eat pigs because that is what you are . . ."

This is something—at last!—that we can agree on with our Muslim cousins. Stop this pig farming and open another cardiology practice!

Your friend,
Moshe

From: moniqueduchene@yahoo.com
To: david.rosenmerck@gmail.com
Date: May 17, 2009
Subject: Tomorrow


David,

I can't manage to get a hold of you.

I'm sorry, but I have to cancel our lunch tomorrow. I fainted this afternoon and the doctor asked me to come in. Nothing serious, don't worry. I've been on a diet and must have taken it a little too far . . .

The result: Elisabeth has invited me to stuff myself at Le Bernardin next week. Hmm . . . roasted chicken at the price of gold. That should do me some good.

Love,
Mom


p.s. I pressed your clothes. Everything is ready for you.

From: Annabelle.rosenmerck@mac.com
To: david.rosenmerck@gmail.com
Date: May 17, 2009
Subject: Daddy's girl


Dear gay brother,

I left Tel Aviv yesterday to go see Dad, but I made a detour to Bethlehem. You know, where we once celebrated Christmas in a life-sized Nativity scene with thousands of people. I'm looking at that Nativity scene right now—cut in two by a never-ending block of cement. I wanted to see this wall—to see if it really existed. I've never felt so bad, David. I'm ashamed that we've done this because it's us, in front of the entire world. Us, the Jews.

The Israelis call the wall *gader ha' harfrada*, which in Hebrew means "a fence of separation." The Palestinians call it *jidar al-fash al-unsuri*, which can be translated to say "a wall of racial segregation."

Over eighty percent of Israeli society supported the construction of the wall. The same people who can never agree with each other! This is the most fractured country in the world! But they came to an agreement. On what? A wall! Imagine the kind of desperation it takes for a population that has only ever experienced rejection and xenophobia to agree on exclusion.

I rented a car and sat in it for three hours, immobile, at a border crossing while the line next to mine moved forward at a regular pace. For no reason. Just to show that they were all-powerful, a few pimply faced Israeli soldiers were humiliating women, old people, and strong men, all with indifference. The atmosphere is oppressive. I'm so sad. When I finally got to the barrier, the guy didn't let me pass. He asked me what I planned to do "in the others' place." I said, "Just see." He said that I might not be able to get back into Israel after, so I got scared. I stayed in front of that wall and cried. A female soldier addressed me with an aggressive tone. I explained to her that I'd come there as a child and that we'd look far off into the distance. Now it's as if the future were dead. She told me that the idea for the wall came after the attack in June of 2001—a Palestinian kamikaze blew himself up in front of a nightclub in Tel Aviv, killing more than twenty people, most of whom were high school students who were just going there to make out. Do you remember? When someone suggested the idea of a wall, everyone jumped on it. We use whatever piece of tissue we can find to wipe away tears, but this one blinded them. "Yes, it's true, there are a lot fewer terrorist attacks," the guard said. "It works, but we're suffocating, too." She told me that sincerely. "We never dream about tomorrow in Israel. We know that we're mortal. But we try."

I don't care about her pain or her toughness. I don't want the country that represents us to be a sealed tomb. I want to break down this wall, blow it up into pieces. I'd like a child's magic marker to draw a door in the wall and open it—and have the entire wall collapse like Legos. Boom. But it's impassable. Where are the hippies? Isn't there a young generation that wants peace? It's easy to say, I know. Jews came here to stop being victims, but we can't seem to manage it.

The Berlin wall was built to prevent people from leaving. The Israeli wall prevents people from getting in.

We're like children snickering, hidden in a cupboard while the big game of hide-and-seek is going on. We've blown it before the start.

I took the road back to Nazareth. What a land of contrasts—from the back of that boy to the faces of the soldiers, and those lines of desperate people paying for the actions of terrorists. They call them "resistants." It's like with the wall—everything is a question of terminology.

Do you remember our picnic at Tiberias, near the lake? And us, with our horrible plastic shoes so we could walk on the rocks? Jellies—isn't that what we called them? The heat of that day—it's one of the first sensations I can remember.

Love,
Annabelle

# From Harry Rosenmerck to Monique Duchêne
Nazareth, May 17, 2009

Monique,

Our daughter has arrived. She's fine, thanks.

I suppose I can explain some things to you now. Before, it would have been complicated—not because I was afraid to, but probably because I didn't understand it myself. Like the storyline of a film that you don't get until the end.

I remember those few days perfectly. And yet, they're like a dark stain in my life. You're not far from the truth when you mention adultery. I was supposed to go away with a woman. She was married, too. We'd been circling each other for a while—I wasn't especially attracted to her, but she excited me. She made me feel desirable. And I'd never felt that way. You loved me, so I made love to you. It wasn't unpleasant, but I didn't feel like you really wanted me, like you wanted to lose yourself in me. Anyway.

We had a rock-solid excuse to go away for a night and a day so we could stay in a little hotel upstate—without the need for any equipment other than a mattress neither of us had used for our respective conjugal slumber.

Her son got an ear infection, so she canceled. I'd already hit the road and was calling to say I'd be waiting for her. I stood there for a long time, staring at the handset in the telephone booth where I'd stopped. It was a gas station in the Catskills. The plan was for me to call you and announce a medical emergency or some heart attack that required emergency surgery. But the whole thing went under, and, by the way, it started to rain.

I stayed in that phone booth for a long time. Maybe a minute—maybe an hour? In any case, it felt like a long time. All the exhaustion of my life came crashing down on me.

I got back in the car and drove all the way to the hotel, robotically, without thinking about the consequences, without considering the possibility of you or the children being worried. I was happy she didn't come. What would I have done with her? Suddenly, even sex disgusted me.

I went to bed and slept. I must have turned on the TV, called for room service. I remember being totally lethargic. After a few days under anesthesia, I finally opened the curtains. Outside, on the gravel of the hotel parking lot, there was an elderly couple. The woman was holding her husband's hand tightly since he was having trouble walking. There was a lot of love in their gestures. The sun burned my eyes. I'd been in the dark for days.

And without formulating anything in my head, I suddenly pictured the end of my life—our old age. I never would have imagined that we would not grow old together, that other lives awaited me.

How could I have explained this interlude to you? In the movies, it would have been a simple fade-to-black. Thank you for not saying anything to me when I came back home.

Judging from our daughter's face, her fade-to-black must have had a nice smile.

Love,
Harry

# From Harry Rosenmerck to Rabbi Moshe Cattan
Nazareth, May 19, 2009

Dear Moshe,

Thank you for the course in porkology. (Do we say that?)

I had a good laugh. Man, you're a smart one!

There is one thing that you certainly don't know and that is that our cousins the pigs have hearts that are compatible with our own. And a few years ago, I witnessed the grafting of a pig's alveolus onto the lungs of a child.

Anti-Semitism will always find roots, you know, with or without seeds!

But the Three Little Pigs continue to whistle in the forest. I'm like them. I'm not afraid of the Big Bad Wolf.

I told my friend Hassan what you said. I asked him what he thought about it. Why is pork forbidden to Muslims? "Why? Because God wanted it that way!" he answered, before adding, "Only you, the Jews, ask yourselves all of these questions."

And he's right. Even you, sir, my good friend, dearest rabbi, aren't satisfied with simply believing. You're looking for a reason.

And so, despite everything, deep down inside, you—like me—know it's all a load of crap.

Harry

New York State Office of Children and
Family Services
Capital View Office Park
52 Washington St.
Rensselaer, New York 12144

Mr. David Rosenmerck
143 West 46th St., Apt 5D
New York, NY 10036

Re: Your application to adopt
File 89008865336

May 19, 2009

Dear Sir,

Upon review of your file, I regret to inform you of the rejection
of your application to adopt.

Despite your numerous positive qualities, we do not feel that
you are able to provide a child with a stable home.

Yours sincerely,
Jennifer Raven

## From Rabbi Moshe Cattan to Harry Rosenmerck
Nazareth, May 21, 2009

Dear Harry,

I just want to tell you that I met the piece of work (who, despite looking like one, isn't a rabbi!) selling those trips to the land of suffering.

Would you believe he drives an Audi convertible?

The exploitation of our memorials seems to be a profitable business. And after the success of Mecca-Cola, our friends on the other side of the wall are selling Muslim Up Lemonade! The laughs aren't over, believe me.

Moshe
(The real rabbi)

# From Annabelle Rosenmerck to Monique Duchêne
Nazareth, May 22, 2009

Mom,

I cannot wait for you to receive this letter. I'm stuck here, without a telephone and no network.

You'll never guess! I was walking around Dad's big house earlier. We can say taking a walk because he bought a kibbutz where twenty people were living! It's like a Texan estate. I was curious about a room that always stays closed. The other night, I saw him hiding the key—he looked like a child. I pretended not to notice and, of course, waited for him to leave so I could take it . . .

This morning he went to see his friend the rabbi. Yes! He has a rabbi friend he plays chess with and discusses pigs and false rabbis and I don't know what else. See how I draw out the suspense? No, Dad isn't Blue Beard, but the room is a kind of museum dedicated to David. You wouldn't believe it. Sixty square meters with newspaper articles all over the walls. His works in every language. Tickets for his plays from all over the world . . . Dad's like a deranged fan.

Mom, I'm begging you, don't tell David. I'm only telling you because I don't know who else to tell. If I tell Lawrence, David will no doubt feel betrayed. I'm worried he'd take it as admiration for his celebrity and not for who he really is. David has always had a problem with that. I fear he'd reject Dad if he found out about this kooky adulation. And then they'd never find each other again . . .

I'm enclosing some printouts of photos I took of the room before Dad came back. Despite the lack of internet, he has a computer and a printer. This place is old-school. At night, you can hear the pigs walking around high up on the platforms. It's like the ghost of Miss Piggy is making the whole house creak. And now he's fighting religious folks who want to destroy his "profane" property. My father is nuts. I truly love him, but I understand why you left him.

See you soon,
Annabelle

# From Monique Duchêne to Harry Rosenmerck
New York, May 27, 2009

Dear Harry,

Your letter did me some good. It's been a long time since we told each other the truth. Now I'll try and take my turn at it.

I always had the impression that the truth was vulgar. That's what I was taught as a child. My father drank too much, was sometimes incoherent, but Mother always insisted that he was simply absentminded. When my grandmother became very sick, she never said anything about it. She kept powdering her cheeks until, at the end, she was painting them—she never let anyone see how ill she was.

I'm like them, but I don't want to be anymore. I want to take off my skin like you take off a bathrobe. At my age I should avoid taking off my clothes as much as possible! And tell the truth. No doubt it would help me know what it is.

Love,
Monique

From: Annabelle.rosenmerck@mac.com
To: david.rosenmerck@gmail.com
Date: May 28, 2009
Subject: The animals the color of my cheeks


Dear David,

Here is proof that Dad is alive. It's a photo I took at sunset. I think he's handsome now that's he gotten older. The second bit of proof is stuck to my cheeks. You wanted them to be pink? Him, too, apparently, since he slapped me as soon as I arrived. It was his way of showing me that he was worried. Refined, as always, and full of gentleness.

I told him he should get a telephone line, that it'd make things simpler. He told me things would be simpler if I got married and let someone else worry about me instead of him. And I thought I was almost done with therapy. It's no surprise his kids are an old maid and a fag.

I came into the center of Nazareth to make a few phone calls and send this email. He's definitely breeding pigs, no doubt about it, unless they're expertly disguised ostriches. I'm going to get a good look tomorrow so I can give you a description worthy of this insanity.

Our father, Harry Rosenmerck, is a pig farmer in Israel. Better get used to it.

I'm on the terrace of a café. I'm dreaming of another extended hand, another Avi. No, that's not true, I'm dreaming of his hand—I'm dreaming of him or the feeling of youth he gave me. He's nobody; but he's an important being in my life, I know it.

Your sister

p.s. I hate that review. Sure, he writes well, but it's bullshit. Your play is powerful and pure. Don't let anyone convince you otherwise. But if you're dead set on screwing him, knock yourself out.

# From David Rosenmerck to Harry Rosenmerck
New York, June 1, 2009

Dear Dad,

When I was little, I always asked you what your "bob" was. Remember? You'd answer, "Cardiologist," and to explain what that was, you told me you were a doctor. It was Mom who finally told me what kind of doctor: one who treats hearts.

It took me years to figure out that the word "heart" referred to an actual muscle containing blood, arteries, and who knows what other real-life, putrid horrors.

I thought you healed lost or broken love. That patients didn't stay unhappy for long. That they just had to come see you.

I gave an interview this morning. A journalist asked me if, like all little boys, I'd ever dreamed of doing the same job as my father. I answered in the negative, without hesitation. I was wrong. In fact, I do have the same job as my father. The one I thought was your job when I was at an age where I admired you unconditionally. I treat hearts with words. I bandage their heartaches with my own. And I make them believe that, somewhere, happy stories exist.

So maybe life will offer me one in return?

Don't you think?

Your son,
David

## From Harry Rosenmerck to Monique Duchêne
Nazareth, June 1, 2009

Dear Monique,

Judging from the photos Annabelle showed me, I think you can shed your clothes without shame.

As for your father, he was an alcoholic *and* absentminded. It would have been difficult for your mother to incessantly repeat, "Excuse my husband, he's an alcoholic." It was better to say he was absentminded. She had common sense.

Annabelle is solitary for a girl her age. She stays in the house and reads for hours. What characters our kids are! I don't really know David anymore, but I've fixed a static image of him in my mind. As for Annabelle, sometimes I recognize the child that she was, but at other times, she escapes me. I keep pretending to be a solid, exemplary father. The truth is our kids keep thinking we can protect them from life, forever.

I didn't understand my father's weakness until I became a father myself. I'm making the best of it. I'm starting to feel old fairly often. More and more often.

Harry

# From Annabelle Rosenmerck to Professor Andrew Black

Nazareth, June 2, 2009

Andrew,

This is a breakup letter—for myself. So I can mourn for my illusions. You stole my youth and I forced you to confront your old age despite being your attempt to avoid it.

Thank God you didn't leave your wife. I won't have to wipe your ass, guiltily, in a white house in Florida where you'll want to croak just like all the old, rich guys.

You think you're sophisticated. You've read books and you know how to choose wine. But you've drunk corked bottles of wine without even realizing it. I used to be moved when you'd gargle in front of the sommelier—to delight the young woman—and give your descriptions of the color, body, and fruit. Yes, you repeat things well, but you don't feel anything. You register without understanding. It's like literature: you teach it, but you'll only ever publish second-rate works with pretentious covers. You explain the great love stories! You give the keys to understanding pain. Jesus! How dare you! What do you even know about love?

Perhaps you understand a few passages from Roth, the ones in which the young student bonks the age-old professor; unless, of course, it's the student who's actually age-old? As for the rest of literature, believe me, you don't understand a thing. My father, the cardiologist, knows hearts better than you do. Incidentally, Schnitzler was a doctor before becoming a writer, and he reinvented the stethoscope. It's by listening to hearts that one becomes a writer. I'm sorry but, beyond this point, your ticket is no longer valid.

Annabelle

p.s. *Your Ticket Is No Longer Valid*, by Romain Gary. Read it.

# From Harry Rosenmerck to Rabbi Moshe Cattan
Nazareth, June 2, 2009

Dear Moshe,

I'm going to try and come see you in a few days. We need to talk and you need to help me. About twenty men came to destroy my farm this morning. There were Jews, Muslims, and Christians. They've found a common cause. They want me to leave. The Jews don't want pigs on Holy Land. They said that pigs won't fix terrorism. The Arabs were in total agreement. They were arguing this together—already, when they're against each other, it's impossible to distinguish one from the other, but can you imagine what it's like when they're on the same side? If I hadn't been afraid for my life, I probably would have laughed. And the Christians, that's the kicker! Would you believe one of the priests from Nazareth thinks I'm living on the vestiges of the home of Christ, Monsignor Jesus of Nazareth, and that I have to give my house to the Church for posterity? They were shouting, "This place belongs to history!"

The priest, a certain Eusebius Martin—Belgian and redheaded—told me I'd be receiving a letter from the Pope! That's right . . . and an offer to buy back the plot of land.

It all seems like a big joke. This country is one. Jewish humor has taken up residence among, and despite, its own.

I hope you are well.

Best,
Harry

# From Rabbi Moshe Cattan to Harry Rosenmerck
Nazareth, June 4, 2009

Dear Harry,

Jesus of Nazareth was a preacher who performed healings using potions—even exorcisms.

He was a Jewish guru, if you like—and, frankly, his sect ridiculed us!

Anyway, the people who practiced this derivative of Judaism were called the "Nazarenes." They simplified things by calling him Jesus "of Nazareth," but the reality is that Nazareth was an abandoned city at the time. Jesus was born in Bethlehem. Everyone agrees on that point. To make up for that, Matthew, in his Gospel, explains that a king wanted to assassinate all of the newborns, so Mary and Joseph had to leave Bethlehem for Nazareth.

There are a thousand interpretations. What is certain is that, at the time, Christians had to endorse the fact that Jesus was a descendant, if not the reincarnation, of King David . . .

So, he had to come from Bethlehem, the city of our king.

The real problem is that historians know that Nazareth wasn't repopulated until the middle of the 1st century of the Christian era, long after Jesus, who was "technically" born long before the year zero. Even the Church doesn't refute these historical realities.

All of this is to say that we have enough troubles as it is without having to suffer the excesses of some loony Belgian priest. Did they break everything? What a bunch of crooks! They have no respect, no dignity. I'll try and calm things down, but you're in a bad position. Have you filed a complaint? Why not raise cows? Or open a medical practice? Or even a *bkeila* restaurant?

Be brave!

Your friend,
Moshe

# From David Rosenmerck to Harry Rosenmerck
New York, June 7, 2009

Dad,

Yesterday, I saw an Israeli film called *Lemon Tree*.

At some point, the Palestinian heroine hears wolves in the valley. I think it's a fairly basic metaphor for Israelis. But is it true, Dad? Are there real wolves in the valley?

Oh God! I fear for your little pigs. Do they live in a brick house?

David

# From Harry Rosenmerck to Rabbi Moshe Cattan

Nazareth, June 15, 2009

Moshe,

I hope your daughter is doing better. Chicken pox is always impressive! I had it very late and believe me when I say it's better that she has it now. (A stupid comment—it would be better if she never got it at all!) It's funny how history creates loops—my daughter Annabelle had chicken pox here, in Netanya. It was the first time I brought my children to Israel. What a terrible memory. The newspapers were reporting on the first crime of pedophilia in the country. It made me waver. Instead of becoming a family, we—the Jews—had become the citizens of a country just like any other. I say "we" because, even far away, I always felt like Israel was my home. I enlisted as a voluntary nurse during the Six-Day War, but it was too short for Israel to need me and I never even got on the plane! During the Gulf War, I was called to duty. I preferred being under the bombs wearing a gas mask to sitting in front of a television.

This morning, I'm reading the news with my heart in my mouth. Did you read about the lynching of that father? He was found dead on a beach. Killed by two Israeli Arabs and two young Jewish women—one of them a soldier in the IDF.

Would I want to take a plane to that kind of country? Is it still my family? What religion protects us from ourselves?

I can't help feeling like I'm in mourning for a cousin and ashamed for the murderers—almost responsible. Israel only has meaning for the diaspora coming here in search of refuge. Those who were born here don't understand the value of the country, which transcends them. They are reproducing the inhumane actions that forced us to create a refuge. And we thought it would remain a refuge. What arrogance! What naiveté! What pretention! Human beings are human beings! We're just like everyone else. May God prevent us from creating our own Hitler just like the Iranians did! Barbarity lies dormant inside each of us—and in me too, no doubt. How am I any different? And that's what paralyzes me—makes me want to scream, cry, and try to help. But what can I do, Moshe? Dear Moshe, I feel sad and old this morning. I fear the world that awaits our children.

Harry

# From Rabbi Moshe Cattan to Harry Rosenmerck
Nazareth, June 16, 2009

Dear Harry,

Only three out of six got the chicken pox. First, I'll care for my little ladybug and then I'll write you back properly. This torrential rain frightens me. In the middle of June, in Israel. And this heat won't break. Between the blisters and the tropical weather, I'm waiting for a swarm of locusts at any time. I must read the Bible too much.

Moshe

p.s. My daughter is scratching. She looks horrible. And I'm a rabbi—I have no Christian compassion.

# From David Rosenmerck to Harry Rosenmerck
New York, June 15, 2009

Dear Dad,

I've started writing a novel—the kind you always called "real writing," not like theatre.

It's the story of a man who didn't catch his train. His whole life was inside it, smiling back at him, but he let it leave with the train. As he watched them—his wife, his children, his life— leave on this train that was going far away, the pain made him feel good. He doesn't think about the train after that. You can't make up for the life that's leaving; you take another path. I wonder if, on that path, my hero will really be himself.

Is there a story? The right story—the one that, once it's told, will silence all of the others?

I live with a dozen notebooks, each half-filled with scribble, and just as many aborted lives.

And soon, Israel. I'm counting down the number of sleeps.

David

From: Annabelle.rosenmerck@mac.com
To: david.rosenmerck@gmail.com
Date: June 15, 2009
Subject: Melody and vodka


David,


It never stops raining. Sometimes I forget where I am. Everything is foreign here. At night, the tapping of pigs' hooves on the wooden platform sounds like a dance.

Click on this link: http://www.youtube.com/watch?v=Ch68o Gw5swg. This music is for you. I composed it on the piano last night.

Do you still write with your headphones on and vodka in your mouth?

I miss you.

Sometimes, I'm overwhelmed by a suffocating nostalgia for those years when we lived with Mom. We threw dance parties. I'm sending you a forty-five that'll make you laugh.

I'm remembering our discussions on the way to school—the detours we took to walk with Jeremy Lucas. I thought you were doing that to make me happy. It took me a while to figure out that you liked him as much as I did!

When I left New York to go and live in Paris, I thought that nothing would be different when I came back.

I wasn't aware that time, which doesn't give a damn, would crush my childhood. That's probably why I have a hard time coming back. You come back to find things you left behind. And I was afraid of our empty rooms and Mom in the silence of that apartment.

Are you happy, David?

Your sister

# From Monique Duchêne to Harry Rosenmerck
New York, June 15, 2009

Dear Harry,

Last night, I spent the evening with David and his fiancé.

I am in tears. It was hard.

I never told you because your rejection of our son prevented me from expressing the slightest pain, but it's strange for a mother to see her son put his hand on that of another man: a man I could have loved; a man our daughter could have touched. I don't know how to express the anguish I'm feeling. Annabelle is convinced that I'm getting what I wanted, like some kind of crazy mother who wanted to be the only woman in her son's life. Maybe that's true? Maybe I'm responsible for the boundaries in his life? And those he's crossed.

I wanted to tell you about it so you wouldn't think I was complicit. I know the sadness you're feeling. But I love David, and I want him to feel protected and accepted, no matter what he does.

Life is short, Harry.

It could be for me. Don't ask me to tell you anything more. I'm going to fight, and it's you I'm thinking about today coming out of Maurice's—Maurice Blet, with whom you were in medical school, apparently. There's an anecdote to be found even in horrible times. Will you be there for David if I don't get better? Will you be there?

Monique

# From Harry Rosenmerck to Rabbi Moshe Cattan

Nazareth, June 17, 2009

Dear Moshe,

Do you think a person loves several times in his lifetime? Do you believe that it's love itself that sustains us, not a particular beloved? That we love continuously, like how we breathe, but with more or less pleasure, or ease, depending on the air, depending on our fears and our problems?

Why do we attach love to desire? Yes, I know what the damned reasons are. And family, and lust. Your religious reasons.

I'm so angry with myself for being a hostage to this Judeo-Christian culture!

You know, as a cardiologist, let me assure you that there isn't the tiniest secret space containing love. So where the hell do we put it?

Harry

# From Rabbi Moshe Cattan to Harry Rosenmerck
Nazareth, June 19, 2009

Dear Harry,

The blisters are now scabs and it's all disappearing like magic. The rain is just a memory, too. I need to water the plants again.

Yes, of course I read the newspapers. I saw that three of our children died on a bus. The terrorist was eighteen years old. I don't know if bags of pig's blood would have changed anything.

I also saw our responses: the tightening of our borders, the wall that seems to be closing in on us as if we've built our own tomb. I'm afraid, Harry, like I always am—and I was born here.

When the Palestinians refused the Camp David agreements—although we were positive we'd see their flag flying over East Jerusalem—we, the Israelis, took comfort in the idea that we were right. Refusing to share was proof that they didn't want peace.

But it isn't that simple. At my office, I sometimes counsel couples that are getting divorced. Men can't appease their jilted wives with a good settlement. It humiliates them. They want something else, but what they're asking for can't be given. They want to leave with a new soul and their illusions intact. The

Palestinians are a proud people; but they're fighting to reclaim something that is dead: the past. Even if they one day claimed all of the land in Israel, they still wouldn't be satisfied.

As for us, we believe that the Palestinians' clumsy and sometimes shameful acts justify our own. David Grossman said that being strong and seeing oneself as weak is a great temptation. We, the all-powerful, with our tanks and our bombs, have convinced ourselves of our weakness and impotence when confronted with the ill will of a betrayed woman. Yes, the Palestinians have been betrayed.

And what if that woman's family stopped pitting her against her ex-husband? If her friends stopped telling her he was a bastard so that, gradually, happier times could bubble up to the surface? Even without marriage, even with distance, like friends, those two people could offer each other a great deal.

Anyway, Harry, I'll stop my rabbinical metaphors. My son leaves for the army tomorrow. The idea that he could have a human target at the end of his rifle makes me nauseous.

I hope we'll see each other soon.

And regarding the question you didn't ask: my answer is that there is no shame in being in love with your ex-wife.

The loop is closed, isn't it?

Moshe

From: david.rosenmerck@gmail.com
To: Annabelle.rosenmerck@mac.com
Date: June 20, 2009
Subject: Adolescence

Dear Annabelle,

Are you on benzos, Prozac, or some other kind of med with an alien name? Jeremy Lucas! He must have a saggy ass and three kids by now.

As for the record you sent, *no comment*. There's always something shameful about the first time. It wasn't the lay itself or the girl. It was my choreography to that song afterward. Even with that, nobody (not even me) figured out that I was gay!

Yes, I'm happy, sometimes. Not too much so. I'm a writer, so that would be counterproductive. I was touched by your music. Quit your studies. Compose. Fuck. Live.

As a result of prolonging your childhood, you're going to die having never become a woman. Take the risk and dive into the deep end. The water is cold, I won't deny it; but you get used to it and, sometimes, you have a lot of fun.

Your brother,
David, who still drinks just as much vodka . . .

# From Harry Rosenmerck to Monique Duchêne

Nazareth, June 20, 2009

Dear Monique,

It's funny, I get the impression I'm just now beginning to understand who you are. Years later. Unless we're molting and you left
your old skin in our apartment on West 26th Street?

We've had two kids. We've loved then hated each other, been
disgusted, then indifferent, and then deeply moved. What are
we to each other? Family? A piece of us that we planted along the
way—lost youth, maybe?

Dear lost youth,

Dry your tears.

Why do you think David's sexuality is your fault? Why blame
yourself? David isn't a victim of the consequences of our actions.
David is David. My reasons for being angry with him are deep
inside of me. I don't think I can reveal them without falling
apart. Love him as he is, and more deeply, because I don't think
I am capable.

We aren't guilty and he isn't sick; he's just different. It's the consequences of that difference that are stuck in my throat as a father, not the differences themselves.

You'll be there. You'll always be there. You're a pain in the ass. And death won't get a hold of you.

Harry

# From Annabelle Rosenmerck to David Rosenmerck
Nazareth, June 26, 2009

Dear David,

It's true, I've got childhood stuck to my shoes.

And real adult heartache that I can't seem to shake—unless it's really just a hideous wound to my pride. Or boredom. One day, I'm going to have to decide to establish some roots. Choose a place, a job, a life, and a man who loves me.

Dad and I are going to Grandma's grave at Herzliya—a kind of road trip. I made a picnic.

Dad has lots of nice employees that take care of the pigs. Most of them are Christian. Tricky for Jews or Muslims to touch pigs . . .

We never talk about the Christians in Israel, but life isn't easy for them either.

Every religion has a different version of history. It's funny and terrifying. Where is the truth buried?

When are you coming, dear brother? I miss you . . .

I'm trying to talk to Dad about you, but the wall seems impenetrable.

Annabelle

# From Harry Rosenmerck to Rabbi Moshe Cattan
Nazareth, June 26, 2009

Dear Moshe,

My apologies for not answering sooner. I am crazy with work.

I liked your analogy of the "betrayed woman." However, the international community has nipped and tucked her to the point of a lie!

When you think that Yasser Arafat received the Nobel Peace Prize! He who only ever knew terrorism, autocracy, and corruption! This Nobel really is a clownish decoration.

The entire world throws stones at the shameful husband that we are. It isn't just kids who'd rather see stones skipped on water than the ones that fall at the feet of our young soldiers, but newspapers all around the world.

Oh yes, it's true, the Palestinians refused to make peace. So what do we do now?

Endure the attacks without responding?

It's a horrible impasse. And over the coffee and cigarettes shared with my Arab friends from Nazareth, we've come to the same conclusion: we all want the same thing. King Solomon has proposed cutting the baby in two—one of us has to bow out in order to stop it!

It's time to be Jewish mothers, to leave. It's the only way to save Israel.

But even if we wanted to, where would we go?

Harry

# From Father Eusebius Martin to Harry Rosenmerck
Nazareth, July 4, 2009

Mr. Rosenmerck,

You dishonor your people by raising pigs on Holy Ground.

We, the representatives of Christians, the Pope, and of Monsignor Jesus Christ, ask you, once and for all, to pack up your belongings and your pigs and leave this land.

That place, the cradle of the world, is the property of God and the Church.

Go in peace,
Father Eusebius, savior of purity

# From David Rosenmerck to Harry Rosenmerck
New York, July 4, 2009

Dear Dad,

Do you remember our summer vacation in Botswana? It was before you and Mom separated—a few months before. What a bizarre vacation. It was winter there. You wanted us to see something different. Other faces. Another way of life. Just before you changed ours forever. We would wake up at dawn to see the sun rise over a foreign land. The day before we left, we saw the Okavango River that crosses Namibia before arriving in Botswana. You explained that, after a geological accident, it gushed into the Kalahari Desert instead of emptying, as it most certainly should have, into the Indian Ocean. People call it "the river that never finds the sea."

I woke up in the middle of the night. I dreamed about you and that river. We were standing together before it. You were describing it to me as if I were a child, but at the same time, you were talking about me. I was the river that never finds the sea. That spills out into the desert. Of course it seems useful—it creates a kind of enormous sea the size of Ireland! It can water whatever it likes. But it cuts off the cycle, and therefore life.

You see, Dad, I do love women. Like you love the lights on Christmas trees. They don't displease me—they even enchant me. But they're not presents for me. My presents come with strong hands and men's faces. Yes, men's faces. That's the way I am. And it's next to a body like mine that I just woke up in tears. I suffer from it, like the river, but I've created something in my own way; I've created art. And you are my source, not the Indian Ocean. I shouldn't be cut off from you. I'm in Israel on the first day of next month. Back to the source, Dad.

David

## From Rabbi Moshe Cattan to Harry Rosenmerck
Nazareth, July 6, 2009

Harry,

It's wedding month and I can't take it anymore. All the tears of joy and piles of wedding cake. I'm getting fatter by the minute.

See, dear Harry, you also victimize yourself.

We've claimed so often that the Palestinians don't want peace that we're now totally convinced of it.

You need only consider the indifference that welcomed the Arab League's proposal for peace in 2002. It's like an overdose of family drama. All of the young Jewish immigrants from Algeria think they need to get revenge on the Arabs who kicked them out, and the Russians who come to the Promised Land bring their fathers' racism with them . . .

Anyway, we're screwed. What are the Arabs trying to tell us? What do we do? I tend to opt for passive resistance, education, and sharing. When my grandmother spoke to me of her native Tunisia, she remembered open doors, dinners at this person's home or that person's home. The Arabs were her cousins.

With love,
Moshe

p.s. Enclosed is a photo of my son Simon in uniform. He looks like a kid dressed in a costume. I can't stop taking pictures of him—probably because I'm terrified of losing him. Not just out of fear that he'll die, but out of fear that his face will change forever.

# From Monique Duchêne to Harry Rosenmerck
La Capelle-et-Masmolène, July 4, 2009

Dear Harry,

I'm at my parents' house—I say that as if they might appear at any moment. Maybe the kids will feel that way about us someday?

Do you remember our first weekend here? Mother had, of course, prepared a pork roast for the first dinner with my Jewish boyfriend. She swore she didn't know that Jews didn't eat pork or that she'd forgotten. I laugh about it now, but it nearly broke us up . . .

The weather is nice here, as always. And the scent of the pines comforts me. Would you believe that La Capelle and Masmolène—two villages that previously loathed each other—now form one continuous town? The town hall was built smack-dab in the middle! The residents still hate each other, despite living in the same town. They only agree on the one thing that unites them: their love for their mayor.

The fig tree you planted looked dead last week. It was on its last leg, nearly on the ground. But I righted it with ropes, as if tying it to life, and dug a hole around its base in which I poured water.

Now, little green shoots have appeared and tiny figs are growing. It wasn't easy to bring it back to life and nothing is certain; but that tree is like me and its roots are planted in the ground of my home. If it grows again and produces fruit, maybe I can, too?

Your tree gives me strength.

I'm going back to New York tomorrow to see David. He'll be in your neighborhood soon . . .

Monique

# From Harry Rosenmerck to Rabbi Moshe Cattan
Nazareth, July 18, 2009

Dear Moshe,

We don't see our sons and daughters grow up. No matter how old they get, we always see them as children. I'm thankful my son doesn't have to play war.

But his mother is sick. She's going to die. I am too, one of these days. I'd like to be able to taste the wedding cake at my daughter's wedding.

I'm troubled this morning. I dreamed about my mother and it was so real.

She told me to reconcile with my son, David. I've never spoken to you about him.

Mother kept saying, "If you don't get up to take him in your arms, I won't come and see you." To which I replied that she was dead. "This is proof that I'm not," she answered. Then she gave me a hard smack that really hurt. This morning, I woke up with a huge red mark on my cheek.

Harry

# From Rabbi Moshe Cattan to Harry Rosenmerck
Nazareth, July 20, 2009

Dear Harry,

Every morning when we wake up, we give thanks to God for giving us his soul out of pure love.

Of course, I'm a rabbi, so I believe that God is in all things. Though I am certain of the existence of the subconscious, I also think that the Eternal sends us indirect signs through our dreams—that he is a part of what we don't know about ourselves.

What was your mother trying to tell you, Harry? In your opinion?

Perhaps you place too much importance on things you thought you'd get out of life that your son is depriving you of? Maybe a tree's roots are as important as the blossoms at the end of its branches? What do you think? And yes, I am genuinely asking you, because this is important.

Moshe

From: Annabelle.rosenmerck@mac.com
To: david.rosenmerck@gmail.com
Date: August 1, 2009
Subject: Emergency


David,

Mom gave me a note to slip into the Wailing Wall. Remember how she told me I was too old to be writing letters to Santa when I was five?! Anyway, I'd almost forgotten about the note, but today Dad and I went to Jerusalem to see Robbi—you know, his friend the bookseller.

I know I never should have read the carefully folded note, but I thought she'd be asking God for something frivolous, like:

- Make it so that I find a man
- I want grandchildren

That kind of stuff . . .

But David, my heart is pounding right now as I write. She asked God to heal her. From what, David? If it's from her heartache or her secrets, it'd still be a funny request.

But what if she's really sick? You should go and see her, David, just to be sure.

I'm actually scared.

Do you remember the first time we went to Robbi's? We walked for hours in the sun and were out of breath when we finally got there. He only had soda water. We hated it, but we drank it anyway.

My throat is tight and I haven't taken a single step. Take care of Mom.

Annabelle

# From Monique Duchêne to Harry Rosenmerck
New York, July 27, 2009

Dear Harry,

I don't know who to turn to. Your God, who became mine? The one of abstraction. The Jewish religion is right not to give him a face. Should we even give him a name?

What remains of our lives? I imagine it's all the little things that decorate bookshelves; the little treasures that prevent you from grabbing a book on the first try. The frames? The class photos? The invitations? The jewelry box painted by little hands that was originally used to package Camembert? The broken Russian dolls? Annabelle's high school diploma? All that's left is the desire to keep on living. The hope for a last embrace, one more affectionate glance. The desire to keep adding treasures to the bookshelf so we can't grab on to the book, the one with the truth.

I'm not going to get better, Harry. And I need you to tell the kids.

Monique

# From David Rosenmerck to Harry Rosenmerck
Newark Airport, August 1, 2009

Dear Dad,

The sky is clear.

Not even a kite.

But they've announced a technical problem and I won't be taking off tonight.

I want to get on a plane, but I'm not going anywhere.

I have to give a conference at the Hebrew University of Jerusalem tomorrow. But nobody cares about that, right?

It's as if the whole world is trying to stop me. As if a thousand protesting feet wanted to trample our story, our reunion. But I'm coming to see you. Without so much as a word, I'll break down your door.

I won't let life just take its course.

David

From: david.rosenmerck@gmail.com
To: Annabelle.rosenmerck@mac.com
Date: August 1, 2009
Subject: Re: Emergency


Annabelle,

I'm just reading your email at the airport. Do I need to turn around?

## From Harry Rosenmerck to Rabbi Moshe Cattan
Nazareth, August 4, 2009

Dear Moshe,

I received a bizarre letter this morning. The anti-pork group, the saviors of purity as they call themselves, are asking to meet at Our Lady of the Fright Church in Nazareth tomorrow.

I don't know the place, but the name is far from inviting. They want us to reach a compromise and apparently have a solution to propose.

I'll write you as soon as I'm back.

I'm sad that I can't invite you to my house for dinner.

I think that between the nuts who want to shut down my farm and the impossibility of inviting you to my desecrated abode, I'll end up throwing in the towel. Especially since you can't exactly say I'm making money! I bet on the golden calf. I'm like a dealer. Every society needs transgression, and my pigs are a reasonable one!

With love,
Harry

# [Handwritten note]

Harry,

I'm slipping this under your door. I hoped I'd find you here. I'm going to try and join you in front of Our Lady of the Fright, but I'm not allowed to enter the sanctuary of another cult. If, by some miracle, you haven't gone, please stay at home!

Our Lady of the Fright Church was built on the hill where the angry Nazarenes wanted to take Jesus to kill him. If we're dealing with the kind of enlightened types we think we are, you may be in danger.

Moshe

# From Harry Rosenmerck to Rabbi Moshe Cattan

Augusta Victoria Hospital, Jerusalem, August 12, 2009

Dear Moshe,

Thanks for the fruit. The prickly pears are fabulous. Luckily, my hands, eyes, and mouth are working properly. The doctors say I'll walk again—that physical therapy will get me back to normal. I don't really believe it, but I work hard in my sessions in the water, especially since the therapist has breasts like the oranges decorating the basket you sent me!

Oh Moshe!

I wanted to thank you. I don't know how to do it face-to-face. The words get stuck.

When I saw you in front of the church just as those loonies were bringing out that immense cross, I knew I was saved. And if I hadn't already been in pain, I would have laughed to see the look on your face when you entered the forbidden place.

I'm a doctor, so I knew I was having a stroke. I told myself, that's it, that's just life . . .

Do you think those maniacs would have crucified me? I think that was their plan. There would have been a trial. Some journalists want to interview me, but I'm trying to avoid it. We're talking full-on Mel Brooks. Thanks, Moshe, you are my friend. I've never had a friend I agreed with so little. I think it's great. You should find yourself a Hamas terrorist pen pal and me a wolf breeder. We'd write each other hilarious letters.

See, even in writing, I hold back my feelings. I joke when I get emotional. And all of the tranquilizers make me tired and I'm getting old and it's almost nighttime . . . I don't want to turn on this purple ceiling lamp that makes my skin look pasty and my eyes heavy.

Thank you.

You saved my life.

Harry

From: moniqueduchene@yahoo.com
To: Annabelle.rosenmerck@mac.com
Date: August 15, 2009
Subject: [no subject]


My Annabelle,

I wish you hadn't found out about everything on the same day. My illness, your father's stroke. How is he?

If you need to stay with him, I can come to Israel. Surely I can find a good doctor there. A Jewish country without a good doctor—now that would be ironic.

You didn't become an orphan from one hour to the next. He's going to get better quickly, you'll see. And me, I'm always surprising everybody. I'm counting on making it to your wedding. On the other hand, no, still no news from David. He's fine, I know it. He just needs time.

I love you very much,
Mom


p.s. Tell me if I should jump on a plane.

From: Annabelle.rosenmerck@mac.com
To: moniqueduchene@yahoo.com
Date: August 17, 2009
Subject: Re: [no subject]

Mom,

You don't "jump" on a plane when you have bone cancer. Unless it's to say goodbye to the love of your life. Is that what you want to do?

Give me a few days to organize things. I found an apartment in Tel Aviv. It'll be easier for Dad.

Our telephone number is 992 5127, if you want to talk to either of us.

I'm interviewing nice ladies to help Dad, then "jumping" on a plane to find a doctor for my mom so I never have to tell her goodbye.

Annabelle

From: Annabelle.rosenmerck@mac.com
To: david.rosenmerck@gmail.com
Date: August 19, 2009
Subject: Answer!


David,

I went to Israel so Dad could protect me, so I could remain a child.

Now I'm responsible for two beings that are descending the mountain that I'm only just starting to climb.

And you, who are already at the top—could you please tell me what there is to see up there?

Just the void? Or the sky close-up?

Annabelle

From: Lawrence.b006@gmail.com
To: Annabelle.rosenmerck@mac.com
Date: August 28, 2009
Subject: S.O.S.


Dear Annabelle,

Since everyone writes each other in this family, I'm going to do the same. It'll give me the impression of being a part of a whole, part of your armored square.

I'm writing because I haven't heard from your brother. I would be lying if I said I was worried about him. I'm worried about myself. I love him with all of my heart and the idea that his no longer belongs to me is tearing me apart inside.

I spoke to your mother. I know he left after she told him about her illness. Of course, that's what made him run away. Because this is running away. Everything is at the house. He left without taking anything or telling me anything.

I can't help thinking that your mother's looming death has pushed David toward life. And that's where I realize that I'm no longer his life.

I don't know who to turn to. Tell me if you hear from him. I see your mother often, Annabelle; she's not doing well. I think she's refusing to get treatment.

You need to come back.

With love,
Lawrence

From: Annabelle.rosenmerck@mac.com
To: Lawrence.b006@gmail.com
Date: August 29, 2009
Subject: My brother

Dear Lawrence,

I understand the pain you're feeling. I haven't heard from David. My brother is a completely free being who slips through your fingers like quicksilver. Have you ever broken a thermometer and tried catching the mercury?

I know he loves you, Lawrence. But before everything else, he writes. Everything is a pretext for writing. He's a vampire. Your story will nourish him and he will nourish your story to create others from it. That's his way of living, of finding his way. He plants little words, strings pearls, and doesn't stop to reread them. He isn't afraid of hurting.

When real life transcends his story, David is lost. He makes up stories on top of it. Builds a château to erase the wave. Without thinking that another is coming.

You, me—nobody counts in those moments.

But in the little box labeled "life" in the middle of his imagination, you have a place reserved. He's left with someone else, yes, and that someone else is him.

Hang in there.

Annabelle

p.s. Yes, I'm leaving my father in good hands (did you know that a stroke paralyzed his legs? Temporarily, I hope) and will be there in two days.

From: Annabelle.rosenmerck@mac.com
To: david.rosenmerck@gmail.com
Date: September 2, 2009
Subject: Life beyond words

David,

I'm scared. Please give me a sign. Mom needs us. You know how she loves you. It's complicated between the two of us. She's angry with me for not being you. I see it in her eyes when I bring her breakfast.

Come back,
Annabelle

# From Annabelle Rosenmerck to Harry Rosenmerck
New York, September 3, 2009

Dear Dad,

You're right; we don't tell each other anything over the phone. We tell each other we've safely arrived, but we don't tell each other the truth.

The truth is that Mom is alone and in terrible shape.

David left without a word. We don't know where he is.

Here is a sonogram. I hope you'll see the family likeness: it's your first grandchild. Yes, you're going to be a grandfather. That's the other truth that I kept silent in Israel and over the damned telephone.

Mom is better just by touching my stomach . . .

Annabelle

## From Harry Rosenmerck to Annabelle Rosenmerck
Tel Aviv, September 5, 2009

Dear Daughter,

I knew by the look in your eyes when you came to my house.

I guess I shouldn't ask about the father, but I am one so I'm worried. Is this a souvenir of the old married man who didn't know how to love you? Or did you fall in love in Nazareth without my knowing?

I think it's love. At least, I hope so.

I'm very happy; but I'd always thought you'd marry first . . .

Dad

From: Annabelle.rosenmerck@mac.com
To: david.rosenmerck@gmail.com
Date: September 6, 2009
Subject: The playwright uncle

David,

Maybe this letter will finally get you to respond. You're going to be an uncle, David. For two months, I've refused to accept the obvious, hidden my heavy breasts under summer dresses, stopped counting the days and the moments of nausea. The father is Avi, the back in the crowd!

This is the perfect example of getting pregnant behind someone's back! My own, especially. Yes, yes, you'll have understood by now that if I'm talking this way, it's because I'm keeping it. I laugh for no reason. I'm completely silly. I keep telling myself I have a bun in the oven, that I'm knocked up, that I'm going to be a whale.

I'm taking care of Mom, but I'm angry with you, David. You're her favorite! You're the one she's always loved. And it's me who's going to have to hold her hand and watch her get smaller and smaller while my belly grows.

Sometimes I feel ashamed. I tell myself that she'll live long enough to see her grandson (yes, it's a boy, I just know it) and that comforts me—I'm transforming my shame into a gift.

I came back to New York on Monday. I don't know when you'll be here. Sometimes, I tell myself that we've seen so little of each other over recent years that we could entrust our correspondence to secretaries and go on just being ghosts.

Dad is getting better. The apartment in Tel Aviv is great. His friend Rabbi Moshe Cattan comes to visit him a lot. The two of them have some good laughs. I'm thinking of the café terrace where Avi took me by the hand, with my hand on my stomach.

Annabelle

From: david.rosenmerck@gmail.com
To: Annabelle.rosenmerck@mac.com
Date: September 9, 2009
Subject: Re: The playwright uncle


Annabelle,

You're going to have the child of a man you don't know! Is this so you can give me a son? To try and win against Mom once and for all? Or to save her? Or to make Dad's heart keep beating?

Think, Annabelle. This child isn't just a symbol. Once he's here, your life will change.

I don't answer because I'm writing a book and I need to forget all three of you—all four of you now—for a little while.

Don't write me.

I love you,
David

## From Monique Duchêne to Harry Rosenmerck
New York, September 12, 2009

Dear Harry,

I never would have thought that pictures of us would make me smile when death looms near . . . I'm looking through our old photo albums. I was pretty and I didn't even know it.

I look like an old chicken carcass now, but Annabelle told me you're coming to see me so I'm making an effort to eat. You always did like plump women . . . And I have a tube of red lipstick close by. That's me—the elegant granny.

So I'm thinking about us in all of this disorder. Remember that time when those Americans invited us to Mustique? We got there to find a huge, empty house and were surprised that no one else was there, that there was no hustle and bustle . . . And then we saw the framed photos and you shouted, "We're at the Lees' house!" He was a shipping magnate who terrified you. We were afraid that someone would see us running away down an alley and got on a plane the next morning! You thought the guy was going to shoot you. As if we'd done something wrong . . .

I don't know why that makes me laugh. Like your need to leave parties when you had to go to the bathroom because you could only go at home . . .

Or your obsession with that little Thai restaurant where you ate the same dish every other day for three years.

And your chess games with Reagan's psychoanalyst over the telephone. You'd wake me up to tell me you'd taken his tower! How did I put up with you?

I'm holding on to memories like an old magpie and telling myself they'll strike a chord with you all the way in Israel.

With love,
Monique

# From Rabbi Moshe Cattan to Harry Rosenmerck
Nazareth, September 18, 2009

Dear Harry,

How are you? I wanted to tell you that Wednesday is Tisha B'Av and you'll need to avoid bathing.

Every year, and you can verify this, it's a perilous date and you'll see the red flag hoisted on the beach. The waves rise by a meter and, unfortunately, people drown.

I think it would be better to avoid going out and instead stay at home and eat. By the way, that's my daily advice! I'm sending you a few *makrouds* that my wife prepared for you.

Have you seen Obama's stance? Clearly, he wants us to take care of this dirty business with Iran so they can play the nice Americans that send provisions to innocent civilians. And so we can officially be the strong arm of the Middle East, whereas we're the only democracy. And I was so moved when the first black American president was elected . . .

Talk to me about politics, Harry. You may run less often, but your brain can still handle a few laps, no?

I'll come over and kick your ass in chess next Thursday. I'd also like to exchange another volume of the Kabbalah for a Philip Roth. I'm reading it in secret at the yeshiva—it gives me a good laugh.

Your friend,
Moshe

p.s. The woman with the strange name who takes care of you—is she pretty? Why don't you ask her to dance?

# From Harry Rosenmerck to Rabbi Moshe Cattan
Tel Aviv, September 20, 2009

Dear Rabbi,

I see that my scathing humor is gradually rubbing off on you (yes, I'm addressing you formally so that you pay me the respect I deserve). Rest assured, the wheelchair in which I spend most of the day is not submersible. But maybe we could make a fortune with little submarines for the handicapped. Their cruel families who want to get rid of them could send them out for an underwater stroll on the cursed day of Tisha B'Av.

I remember this festival that so terrified my grandmother. Like everything else on our calendar, it's calculated based on the position of the moon, which regulates the tides. It's actually an astrologer's religion. I'm going to call you Madame Sunshine, dear Moshe.

So, Moshe Sunshine, how are you? As for me, my ex-wife is dying, and it seems we love each other a little again, remotely. Now that death is just around the corner . . .

My daughter is going to have a child. I don't know whose. I suspect every single one of my pig farm employees. All of my pigs are now either on plates or in supermarket aisles. I don't want to go back to the farm, not to Nazareth or to what I thought was my home. As for my son, at least he'd been useful to his mother, but he's disappeared ever since she got sick. It's a bad made-for-TV movie.

Luckily, I have Laitrockva, whom my daughter found, and she is as ugly as a mud fence, if you want to know the truth. She makes feasts for me so I just eat and eat.

And you, dear Moshe Sunshine? What about you? Any news in your parish? Any signs of the second coming? Is the sea going to part in two anytime soon? All of that interests me.

I walk a little more every day. I hope there are miracles in the Holy Land. I plan to run the New York Marathon in six months, sponsored by a sausage brand, so if things don't start moving faster, I'll have to go to Lourdes. Come see me. Laitrockva will grill us some red mullet and we'll play cards—enough with chess, I'm too good for you.

My best wishes to your nut-busting wife. I'm preparing a good Roth for you.

Your friend,
Harry

p.s. Any news from your son the soldier?

# From Annabelle Rosenmerck to Harry Rosenmerck
New York, October 1, 2009

Dear Dad,

I hope the fat woman with the unpronounceable name is being nice to you and that you're forcing yourself to walk a little. Soon, everything will be back to normal and you can launch a business raising Burgundy snails. It fits all of your criteria, no? It's neither kosher nor halal. It's repulsive and you could run after them.

I'm trying to joke whenever I can, laugh at anything possible. The more steps you take, the fewer Mom is able to. If you could only see her. She's so thin she could break. And my belly just keeps getting rounder. I have the horrible feeling I'm stealing life from her to nourish my baby.

I've only gotten one email from David in two months and he isn't talking to Mom. I'm no longer sure whether she's dying from cancer or the absence of her son. All I know is that she's a shadow and her humor is growing like her clothes—some of them fall off of her now.

I'm going to send you the results from her blood tests. You'll tell me the truth, right? I get the impression the doctors are lying to me, protecting me. Some say a year, others don't want to say anything. But everyone is talking about the end.

She talks about you, you both, like they were the best years of her life. She wants to eat in kosher restaurants. She's forgotten your fights and all of the rest. She's knitting for my baby. She's rereading Bukowski till her eyes ache. "It's my indulgence," she says.

See you soon, Dad,
Annabelle

# From Harry Rosenmerck to Monique Duchêne
Tel Aviv, October 5, 2009

My Monica,

Last night, I dreamed I took you dancing. You were wearing a skirt and I could walk with no problem. I even did a tap solo.

I'm praying because I'm closer to God than you are. I asked him to heal you and I swore to him that if he did, we wouldn't say anything to anyone. We wouldn't write a bestseller or even share an anecdote at dinners in town.

Ah, the dinners in town . . . it's been centuries. Do you remember all the fatally boring parties with my colleagues in New York?

You always wore high heels—you were so pretty. I'd try to lift your skirt in elevators and you'd laugh. We never did anything; we didn't want to be late or be caught in the act. And on the way back home, it was too late. It's always too late on the way home. We've been drinking. We're married. Everything will still be there tomorrow . . .

And here I am, now, a prisoner to these old legs and far away from you.

If I'd only known. If I'd only understood that this was life. You know, in God's eyes, you are still my wife. We didn't divorce religiously. So come on, Monique. Stop the playacting. I can still get a hard-on with Viagra and I've always found you attractive. You're just pretending to be sick to get me back, aren't you?

You drive me nuts like nobody ever could, but God I like you.

There's a lot of God in this letter; I promise it won't happen again.

Your Jewish husband,
Harry

From: moniqueduchene@yahoo.com
To: Annabelle.rosenmerck@mac.com;
david.rosenmerck@gmail.com
Date: November 10, 2009
Subject: Sleep

My children,

I've had my share of sorrow in life and I've had my share of joy.
When I became a mother, my life took on an entirely different
meaning.

I've done everything I can to leave you traces of who I am so that
you can find the pieces to your own puzzle. I've thought so many
times that I am leaving too soon, before I could leave you an
instruction manual for life. It was my lifetime quest to find
happiness for you, to find the formula that would bestow smiles
on your faces, always.

David, Annabelle, the idea that your names will keep echoing
in an empty room reassures me and crushes me at once. When
your father and I divorced, and you spent nights at his house, I
would lie in your beds and imagine that I was stroking your
hair, hushing you to sleep, while you slept under his roof. I
imagined that somehow you could feel it from afar, and that it
calmed you.

Surely I was fooling myself; I was the one who fell asleep imag-
ining your warm bodies near my own. Wherever it is I'm going,

I'll think of you. And every night you'll feel my hand on your hair, that's a promise.

All my love,
Mom

## From Rabbi Moshe Cattan to Harry Rosenmerck
Nazareth, November 27, 2009

Harry, I rang your doorbell. You know that. I heard you crying through the door, even if you didn't make a sound. Even if you shed no tears.

Do you want me to go to Paris with you? Annabelle is keeping me informed. I know things aren't going well.

Life isn't the straight line we imagine as children; it makes loops. We never love by chance. Even if we talk about mistakes, even if we ask how and why, deep down we know why.

When we stop loving someone, it's because we change and mourn a part of ourselves. Like how we love finding an old jacket we haven't worn for ten years and it still fits—we can also find an old part of ourselves.

I think that's what happened with Monique's illness—you both found an old part of you, but death is near, waiting to take it away from you. That's it. A whole part of you is going to die with her.

I am your friend, Harry.

Especially now that you no longer breed pigs.

I am here.

Moshe

From: Annabelle.rosenmerck@mac.com
To: david.rosenmerck@gmail.com
Date: November 16, 2009
Subject: Anger

I'm writing you even though you've forbidden it. It isn't for you to forbid me from writing you. You can't throw people's love away. You're like Dad, actually: you close the door when things don't please you.

And standing in front of that door are Lawrence and Mom—who is dying, David! And I'm there, too, with a child in my belly. That I'm not having for you or against Mom.

I need to start living someday and you have to let me do it. I'm angry with you for leaving me alone with Mom. Do you know what illness is, David, when it gallops, when it goes faster than the things you have to say?

I don't give a damn about the words you're lining up, however beautiful they may be! They're your prison.

I'm asking you to come home. Mom is suffering. She has pain-killers, but no real treatment. It's too late.

The cancer is everywhere.

And it's with you, too, wherever you are. You're only escaping the odors, the rashes, and the sores. Reality is with you, David. I know it.

Annabelle

# From Monique Duchêne to Harry Rosenmerck
New York, November 20, 2009

Dear Harry,

While the light is fading, I want to laugh! It's probably these pills they're giving me. Yes, I'd like to dance. With you. Alone, too. A furious twist, like when I was young. Whenever I think of myself, I'm always twenty.

That would be the beginning of my psychoanalysis, if I ever started it. But I'm always afraid of missing appointments, you know, and I don't think I can guarantee making it for the next.

It's here, Harry. It's all around me. And it's a lot less terrifying than I thought. I don't know if we'll see each other again, but we've already found each other.

Monique

## From David Rosenmerck to Monique Duchêne
Marrakesh, December 1, 2009

Dear Mom,

Yes, no news for four or five months. Ever since you told me you were sick. It's contradictory. I should have stayed. I should have melted into you like a child, taken advantage of our limited time together. But instead, I ran away.

I don't know why. I'm not like Annabelle, capable of analyzing everything. I follow my actions and my instinct. I holed up in a hotel, ruined myself in the minibar. I wrote incessantly. I didn't get in touch with Lawrence either. He must have contacted you. Maybe I wanted to go on being the child everyone worried about? I didn't want to see you wasting away. I didn't want to wipe your ass at the hospital and tell you your wig looks great.

I wanted to be free, free of you, Dad, and Annabelle. I suppose that's impossible. You are my prisoners and I am yours. We are a family. A family that writes each other, that doesn't touch, that doesn't breathe in aromas from the kitchen, but a family nonetheless.

How are you? Who is taking care of you?

It's still strange, this announcement of the end. Yes, we knew it anyway; but it's the countdown that is so violent. One year. A year at best. I have eleven months to no longer be a son, to become your father, to pardon this silence.

I didn't take the plane for Israel. I didn't stay with myself either—I ran from everything and everyone.

There's the truth.

I went out tonight for the first time in a long while. I'd almost forgotten what city I was in! I took a hit from the heat. I've been living in air-conditioning. The odors, the faces, everything over-whelmed me and I cried, Mom. Like a child being born. Your child that is going to have to cut the cord that connects us. I was born again tonight. I'm a real bastard, aren't I? I should help you, tell you you're going to be all right. Take you around the world to see the leading specialists, look through our photo albums, make your favorite foods, and convince you to fight:

"You're going to fight. You're going to get better."

That's what they say in the movies, right? I wish I'd been a movie hero and that we'd won in the end.

Here are the photos of your child who is coming back to you.

See you tomorrow,
David

## From Annabelle Rosenmerck to Harry Rosenmerck

New York, December 2, 2009

Dear Dad,

As I told you on the phone yesterday, Mom died during the night. You didn't say anything, didn't respond at all—are you OK? I can't seem to get a hold of you now. She went quickly, painlessly. Dr. Maurice Blet, who you know, really helped us a lot. David returned from Morocco this morning, almost as skinny as her, as if he'd been carrying her troubles, walking in her footsteps. He thought she'd take him in her arms. He never imagined she'd disappear so quickly, that this was real. He is distraught, Dad, like a child. Even far away, elsewhere, he was always closer to Mom than I ever was.

I can get your plane ticket, if you want to come to the funeral. I'm staying active, organizing things so I can remain standing. I keep telling myself I'll cry later. After . . .

My baby comforts me from within. He makes me strong. Talk to me, Dad. I need to have noise around me. Mom's apartment is so empty. I don't dare touch her things. I asked Moshe to come and see you. I don't know if you're handling the shock. Or maybe it's not such a big deal for you? Like all children of divorcés, I always imagined you still loved each other.

Annabelle

# From Harry Rosenmerck to David Rosenmerck
Tel Aviv, December 1, 2009

David,

When the telephone rang and Annabelle told me your mother had died, I walked to the bathroom, locked myself inside, and sobbed.

The last tears I cried were at your birth, and they ran with joy. I didn't cry for my mother, but I cried for yours.

I managed to walk away from that phone call without thinking, though for days my legs have barely supported me. Now I finally sit to write you with the help of a friend who is forcing me to survive. We all have strengths we're not aware of, as well as sorrows. It's to you I write, it's to you I turn. You, to whom I haven't spoken in more than six years. One day, you become the child of your children. That day has come.

I imagine your pain and your remorse at having not seen your mother in her last few days. I understand what you did. We can't accept that those we love are mortal. I did the same thing with you. I decided that none of it was real; that the David you imposed on me only existed for others—that my David wasn't gone.

In my mind, David is married to a beautiful blonde woman. In my mind, David has a son and I bounce him on my knee. In my mind, David is a doctor and we play chess together. I think I know what makes him tick, but he beats me every time. In my mind, David doesn't kiss other men on the mouth. But in my mind, David is a man without conviction.

My mind is full of regrets, and time is far too short. I was angry with you, and I'm still angry with you. I'm angry with you because my mother emerged from the camps where my father died. She carried me in the face of horror. The sickly infant I was had to struggle to survive. Then I brought you into this world so you could stop everything right here?

It's as if you don't want to fight death and the end of our family name. But who gives a damn, right? Who cares about the names? The survivors? Because they die, too. Everything comes to an end. Including me. Especially me.

I'll be there Thursday for the kaddish. To put the one I loved in the ground. I'll protect you and your sister under the tallit of a father. And soon all three of you. Because Monique isn't with us anymore but another is due to arrive.

Forgive me, my son.

My silences, David, made the sound of love.

Dad

# A Note on the Author

AMANDA STHERS was born in Paris and lives in Los Angeles. She is the bestselling author of ten novels; *Holy Lands* is her American debut. She is also a playwright, screenwriter, and director. Her debut English-language film, *Madame*, was released in the United States in 2018. In 2011, the French government named her a Chevalier (Knight) in the Ordre des Arts et des Lettres, the highest honor it bestows on artists, for her significant and original contributions to the literary arts.